"So sue me for having a prurient streak."

Tempest had *so* not been flirting with Wes.

Had she?

Forcing herself to consider the notion, she wondered if her sexual impulses could conspire to act without her explicit permission. What if her artistic persona and businesswoman facade hid a decadent and determined inner seductress?

Frustrated with the undeniable attraction she felt for a man she probably had nothing in common with, she forged ahead. "Look, I'm sorry if it seemed like I was coming on to you. The dating profiles happened to intrigue me."

"So you're saying your sudden interest in threesomes didn't have a damned thing to do with me?"

"Correct."

Wes grinned. As slow, sexy, I'm-going-to-have-you grin that sent a sensual shiver down her spine. "Good. Because I'm not the kind of guy who likes to share."

Blaze™

Dear Reader,

As I thought about what I wanted to write for my ninth Harlequin Blaze release, I kept thinking about my very first two Harlequin Blaze novels. Both stories—*Silk, Lace & Videotape* (Blaze #26) and *In Hot Pursuit* (Blaze #48)—took place in New York City, with cop heroes working in the same NYPD precinct in Manhattan. I love glittering, glitzy New York for its one-of-a-kind personality. I also truly admire the nobility of men and women who are called to serve and protect. So as I thought about a way to bring a sexy, suspenseful story to the page, I naturally decided to revisit a place teeming with steamy potential for *Silk Confessions,* the first in my ongoing WEST SIDE CONFIDENTIAL miniseries. Wesley Shaw is on the trail of a killer, but first he'll have to get past a sizzling suspect and all the mayhem she leaves in her wake.

I hope you enjoy the new series as much as I loved writing it! And keep your eye on Wes's partner, Vanessa Torres. Her story will be coming in May 2005. Until then, visit me at www.JoanneRock.com to learn more about my future releases.

Happy reading,

Joanne Rock

Books by Joanne Rock

SILK CONFESSIONS

Joanne Rock

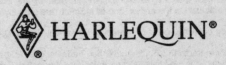

HARLEQUIN®

TORONTO • NEW YORK • LONDON
AMSTERDAM • PARIS • SYDNEY • HAMBURG
STOCKHOLM • ATHENS • TOKYO • MILAN • MADRID
PRAGUE • WARSAW • BUDAPEST • AUCKLAND

ISBN 0-373-79175-5

SILK CONFESSIONS

Copyright © 2005 by Joanne Rock.

Printed in U.S.A.

Dear Reader,

An Evening To Remember... Those words evoke all kinds of emotions and memories. How do you plan a romantic evening with your guy that will help you get in touch with each other on every level?

Start with a great dinner that you cook together. Be sure to light several candles and put fresh flowers on the table. Enjoy a few glasses of wine and pick out your favorite music to set the mood. After dinner take the time to really talk to each other. Hold hands and snuggle on the sofa in front of the fireplace. And maybe take a few minutes to read aloud selected sexy scenes from your favorite Harlequin Blaze novel. After that, anything can happen....

That's just one way to have an evening to remember. There are so many more. Write and tell us how you keep the spark in your relationship. And don't forget to check out our Web site at www.eHarlequin.com.

Sincerely,

Birgit Davis-Todd
Executive Editor

For Pam Hopkins, a wonderful agent,
a patient listener and fearless champion of my dreams!
Thank you so much for your support.

1

TEMPEST BOUCHER had a multimillion dollar corporation to run, a kickboxing class to attend, a board of executives in upheaval and a lecture waiting to be written for a finance seminar she'd promised to give at New York University in a few weeks. But every last bit of it was going to have to wait since *Days of Our Lives* was on in five minutes.

"Eloise!" Juggling her ten-speed bike and the dog leash as she searched for the keys to her building's front door, Tempest whistled to her two-year-old German shepherd. Her spoiled pet seemed utterly unaware of the need to hurry as she gave her best poor-hungry-me look to a corner pretzel vendor in the Chelsea section of Manhattan. Thanks to a new construction site three buildings over, West 18th had suddenly become a prime location for anyone pushing a food cart.

Oblivious to Eloise's irritated owner, the hot-pretzel man tossed the conniving canine a treat. Only then did Eloise deign to obey commands and follow Tempest through the front door. So much for obedience school training.

Tempest grumbled as she repositioned the bike

for the trudge up three flights of stairs. She only indulged her soap opera habit on Fridays, for crying
out loud. Couldn't Eloise fulfill her inner panhandler
on any other day of the week?

Determined to wring some fun—and some sense
of normalcy—out of a life overflowing with
responsibilities, Tempest had made a New Year's
resolution to start living her own life this year. Not
every day was her own, of course. After her father's
unexpected death eight months ago, the task of overseeing day-to-day operations at Boucher Enterprises
had fallen on her shoulders as temporary CEO, taking up most of her time.

But one day a week—Friday—could be hers. For
two months now, she had been spending the weekends at the new studio apartment in Chelsea, a run-
down and wonderfully normal place where none of
her neighbors had noticed the daughter of eccentric
corporate scion Ray Boucher in their midst.

And that was just the way Tempest wanted it.

She'd taken so much pride in finding the space
on her own and paying for it out of a budget from
her meager income as a sculptor. In fact, budgeting
a life in Manhattan on a small income took as much
financial savvy as running Boucher Enterprises.
Possibly more, since the family corporation had a
fleet of accountants and financial analysts whenever she needed a business consultation, whereas
she had no help with her personal finances. Unless
she categorized Eloise's begging on the streets as
"help."

Hustling the last few steps to her apartment door,

Tempest could already hear the opening bars of music for her soap opera in her mind.

"Like sand through the hourglass..."

Days of Our Lives reminded her to slow down. Enjoy herself. The sand through the hourglass had become her personal transition moment where she left behind Tempest the heiress, who had a schedule so packed she needed—good God—an administrative assistant. This was her time to be Tempest the woman who was passionate about sculpting, soap operas and saving her pennies for a future that wouldn't include running the family company.

But as she moved to put her keys in the lock, she realized the door was already slightly open. Had the superintendent finally decided to fix her broken shower?

Sure that had to be it, Tempest chose to let Eloise go first, just in case. Setting her ten-speed on the landing outside her door, Tempest motioned to the dog. Perhaps feeling compliant after her bonus lunchtime feeding, the shepherd dutifully nudged the door open with her snout.

And revealed Tempest's tiny haven, trashed beyond recognition.

NYPD DETECTIVE WESLEY SHAW didn't normally pay any attention to the calls taken by other officers at his precinct on West 20th, but as he meandered past a throng of desks to start his day, a name slowly repeated by a rookie cop caused a flash of recognition.

"Did you just say Tempest Boucher?" Wes leaned

down into Carl Esposito's line of sight, his cop radar blaring an alert.

Ignoring him, Carl continued to copy down information being given to him over the phone.

Wrenching around to peer above the rookie's shoulder, Wes experienced the rush of instinct that always prickled inside whenever he had a good lead—a professional thrill for the chase that he hadn't enjoyed during the two years since his first partner had gone missing. He'd been functioning on autopilot for so damn long, the electric rush was as unexpected as it was welcome.

He'd been coming up empty on a murder case for a week until he'd connected the victim to an online dating service two days ago. And although he hadn't been able to track down anyone at MatingGame.com, he had discovered the business was one of many owned by the successful Manhattan-based conglomerate, Boucher Enterprises.

Seeing Tempest Boucher's name surface in his precinct so soon after his discovery couldn't be coincidence.

"I'll take it." Wes snagged Carl's notes as the officer hung up the phone, determined to follow any lead that gave him the feeling his old partner Steve had called the cop "buzz." Better than your run-of-the-mill Budweiser high, the cop buzz hit your system with the kind of adrenaline surge that solved cases and caught bad guys.

Highly addictive stuff. And Wes had ached for it like a junkie for twenty-four godforsaken months. No way would he let it pass him by now.

"You sure?" Carl reached for his jacket. "I live two blocks from there. I can ask some of the locals if they've seen anything."

Wes was already halfway out the door. "Send a patrol car to meet me. I've been meaning to talk to this woman anyway." He shoved through the double doors into the afternoon gloom when he remembered he needed to inform his new partner.

Yeah, *new*. Vanessa would love that one. She'd been on his back like a bossy sister to pull himself together ever since they'd been paired up eighteen months ago. Jogging back inside, he shouted to Carl. "When Vanessa gets in, do me a favor and tell her where I am."

Ten minutes later, Wes arrived at an address that didn't look anything like the sort of elite building a filthy-rich real estate heiress ought to own. A patrol car already sat out front, attracting some attention from the locals. A few rubberneckers bought hot pretzels from a nearby vendor as if to settle in for any hints of news about what might have happened in the run-down, ten-story building.

Despite New Yorkers' reputation for minding their own business, Wes had yet to see any signs of the phenomenon in nine years on the force.

Making quick work of the stairs, he hit the third floor in no time. A bicycle leaned forgotten in the hall while a woeful-looking black-and-brown German shepherd stood guard at the half-open door to apartment number 35. A skinny old woman clad in a blue-and-yellow floral housecoat watched over the proceedings from number 39, but other than that, the third floor remained quiet.

Pausing to gain the approval of the shepherd, Wes scratched the dog's ears before following a dull hum of voices from inside the airy studio apartment. Light spilled in from floor-to-ceiling windows, illuminating a profound mess of strewn clothing, plants dumped out of their containers and piles of broken statuary. Two uniformed patrol officers were on the scene—one who knelt in the rubble taking fingerprints off some broken glasses and the other who stood near the windows taking notes as he spoke with a petite brunette.

Wes recognized Tempest Boucher from the newspapers. She possessed eye-popping curves and seemed to be rocking back and forth on her heels, perhaps an attempt to calm herself since she looked a little shaken. Jittery.

With creamy pale skin and chin-length brown curls, she wore running shoes with a sleekly cut crimson pantsuit that appeared tailor-made for her lush hourglass figure. Something about her extravagant curves and full red lips brought to mind the cartoon image of Betty Boop, except the apartment owner lacked the wide-eyed look of an ingénue. Her tawny gaze was sharp and assessing.

And preoccupied with him as he bent to retrieve a broken piece of statuary.

"Ms. Boucher?" He noted her stare strayed to the broken piece of clay in his hand. Peering down at the object, Wes discerned a ridge along the top of the foot-long shaft of clay. Only then did he realize the piece he'd recovered was actually a penis.

Reacting on pure male instinct, he dropped the

busted piece back on the couch in all due haste. No cop buzz in the world seemed potent enough to make him seek out clues that damn badly.

"Please, call me Tempest." A hint of amusement fled through her honey gaze, although she didn't halt her nervous rocking. She reached for a choker around her neck, a band of silver-gray velvet with a big chunk of smoky quartz crystal dangling just below the delicate hollow at the base of her throat.

"Detective Wesley Shaw." He reached to shake her hand and realized he was eager to touch her. An irritating thought when she might be mixed up in something dangerous. Deadly, even.

Nodding to the note-taking officer, Wes silently took over the questioning. While he sympathized with this woman, if she were truly innocent, he couldn't allow her to bamboozle one of the new guys just because of her famous face and obvious sex appeal. Skinny Paris Hilton had nothing on the more elusive—and deliciously curvy—Tempest Boucher.

"Would you like to sit down?" He gestured to the couch strewn with sketchbook drawings of hands, feet, arms and—damnation—more penises.

While Wes knew he had no business judging her on the contents of her ransacked apartment, the cop in him couldn't help but wonder if the uptown heiress used this downtown address as a love nest. Or something even more sordid.

Her connection to his murder case linked her with some very unsavory characters.

"Sure." She sprang into action, brushing aside

the smashed figures and hastily scooping up the anatomical drawings. "Have a seat."

A shiver passed through him as her thumb skimmed the base of a pencil-and-ink penis. A wholly inappropriate reaction. How the hell long had it been since he'd had a woman in his bed if he was getting turned on at work?

He would have made a mental note to call his girlfriend of the month, except that this was one of the many months he didn't happen to have one. In fact, if memory served, he'd only managed to accomplish the girlfriend-of-the-month feat twice in the last year and a half. Hell of a track record.

Since he'd always sucked at relationships—something he sorely regretted telling his new partner—Vanessa liked to hassle him about one month being the longest he could keep a woman in his life. Damned if she hadn't been dead-on accurate. Wes didn't bother to inform her that he'd had a long-term interlude back in the day—before his first partner went undercover and never came back out. His job and his personal life had both pretty much fizzled since then. Even more so after they'd finally found Steve's body in the East River last fall.

Rogue thoughts of the sexy socialite now firmly under control, Wes dropped onto the small pullout sofa a few feet away from her. Too late he realized the open studio apartment contained no bed, meaning she must sleep *here*. Right on this very piece of furniture where he'd parked himself.

Eager to maintain focus on his case, Wes redirected.

"Is that your dog out front?"

"Eloise?" She peered around the apartment as if she'd only just remembered she had a dog. Inserting two fingers between her lips, she blew a piercing note.

Wes barely heard it since his eyes were glued to her full mouth, her bottom lip still damp from her whistle.

The dog came padding through the rubble of the apartment, its presence seeming to relax Tempest. "Yes, she's mine. I would never bring a shepherd into the city since they really like to run. But I found her in a Dumpster on the way to work one morning and what else could I do? I figured living with me— even if I don't have a few acres for her to romp around—had to be better than the fate she was looking at."

Wes watched her scratch the dog's neck, her shiny red manicure disappearing into the animal's thick ruff. There was no doubt in his mind the mutt had it made.

"She looks pretty well-adjusted." He didn't mention his St. Bernard was twice the size of Eloise and managed to keep entertained in Wes's shoebox of an apartment on Roosevelt Island. "Can you tell me what happened here today?"

"I was coming home from a meeting and I noticed the front door was unlocked." Her fingers buried deeper into the dog's fur. "Eloise went in first because I was a little unnerved by the open door. I had safety measures drilled into my head at an early age, and I can assure you, I've never forgotten to bolt a door in my life."

"Is anything missing?"

"I honestly haven't looked around. I called the police as soon as I saw the mess." Her eyes drifted over the debris. "I'm not sure I'd know where to start looking for missing items."

Wes followed her gaze, his eyes slowing on a haphazard pile of lacy undergarments spilling out of a tall armoire. Black ribbons mingled with pink straps, bright blue satin billowed over yellow see-through netting. He'd have to be a dead man not to notice the distinctly feminine intimate apparel, but he refused to envision Tempest wearing any of the slinky outfits.

Although the thought tempted him. Mightily.

As a compromise, he told himself he would not only work on finding another girlfriend in the very near future, but he would also seek out one who had a taste for lingerie. Of all the times for his libido to make a comeback after staying in hiding for months.

"Consider if you have anything here that someone else really wants. Something with monetary value? Something with significant value to a particular person?" He studied her face for hints of guilt or subterfuge, but only found deep thought. "The level of destruction in the apartment indicates that the perpetrator conducted a thorough search for something specific, or else the person responsible holds a personal grudge."

His thoughts ran to the old lady neighbor he'd seen peering out her apartment door earlier. Had she been monitoring the goings-on in the hallway for reasons beyond general nosiness? Maybe some of

Tempest's neighbors didn't appreciate the inevitable media frenzy that followed young, beautiful socialites around New York.

Wes found himself wondering if she brought a lot of men back to this apartment. Was the unassuming address her rendezvous point for booty calls she hid from her ritzy family?

"Obviously my intruder didn't think my sculptures were worth a damn." She clutched the smoky crystal at her neck and Wes spied the rapid beating of her pulse there.

What would it be like to make this woman's heart pound faster?

"You collect statues?" Of naked men?

Perhaps Tempest's snooping neighbor was an old prude who resented anyone with such an obvious interest in male nudity.

"I am the artist." She lifted her chin with vaguely injured pride. "I had been hoping to convince a local gallery to do a showing once I had enough of a collection, but now…"

Certain a wealthy heiress whose face frequently graced the social pages could buy her way into any gallery she chose, Wes wasn't too concerned. He needed answers from Tempest Boucher and he certainly wasn't getting them by being subtle.

Time to be a bit more relentless with his questions.

"Did you keep valuables here? Jewelry? Other artwork besides your own?"

TEMPEST STARED BACK at Detective Heartless Shaw and assured herself he must not have a creative bone

in his body. How else could he ask her something so
insensitive as whether or not she owned any artwork
that was actually *worth* something?

Of all the damn nerve.

"As a matter of fact, my statues were the most
valuable items here. I don't keep much at the apartment besides the tools for my sculpting." And a few
pictures for inspiration. Could she help it if she liked
to mold male bodies? Judging by what her first few
pieces had sold for, she wasn't the only woman who
appreciated a naked masculine torso around the
house.

Detective Shaw might actually make for great
male inspiration himself if he didn't have such
abrupt crime-scene manners. With his close-cropped
dark hair and classic Roman features, he possessed
a timeless appeal women would have found irre-
sistible in any era, though his dove-gray eyes and the
hint of a dark tattoo curling around one wrist gave
him a uniqueness she wouldn't confuse with any
other classically handsome male. He wore a vintage
suit that had probably cost a fortune in its prime, but
the threads had seen better days, settling into softer
lines around angular shoulders.

Definitely the sort of shoulders a woman
wouldn't mind molding. In clay, of course.

He peered around her apartment as if to test the
truth of her assertion that she only came here to
work. Curse the man and his unwanted sex appeal.
Wasn't she the victim here? Shouldn't he make a
passing effort to ask her if she was okay? She'd
never been a paranoid woman, but it seemed as if

even the toughest of chicks would be shaken by the sight of their personal lives churned through a giant blender and spit out like an aftertaste all over the floor.

"As soon as we've finished collecting evidence, we need to do a thorough walk-through to see if anything's missing. In the meantime, I've got some other questions I'd like to ask you about Boucher Enterprises." His gray eyes slid back to her, fixing her with unsettling directness. And something more? She could almost imagine a hint of male interest there. Then again, she could be dabbling in big-time escapist thinking to drool over Wesley Shaw instead of focusing on the criminal act some scumbag had committed against her.

"You recognized the name?" She had rather hoped he wouldn't want to discuss her connection to the famous family, but no doubt reporters would have jumped on the police report the moment it was filed anyhow.

Her misfortune would be all over the papers and would certainly prompt more irritated phone calls from her mother about the need to move back to the safety of the family's Park Avenue building on a full-time basis. The media would discover the location of her weekend hideaway and make life in Chelsea impossible. And then there would be the outcry from the Boucher board of directors who never understood her desire to have a life separate and distinct from her commitment to the company.

"There aren't many people in New York who

wouldn't. *The Post* ran a feature on you just a couple of weeks ago—"

"I remember." How could she forget the story that implied she had a fixation with younger men? As if her last-minute decision to go to the cinema with the barely-legal performance artist who ran a coffee shop around the corner counted as a date. "Can we move on to your questions, please?"

Adopting her best all-business demeanor, she dismissed the topic, unwilling to think about what kind of man she would have rather been dating than the coffee guy. Tempest might not enjoy her role in Boucher Enterprises as a corporate bigwig, but that didn't mean she couldn't play the part when necessary. After coming home to a trashed apartment, finding her last year's worth of work destroyed and missing *Days* to boot, she wasn't really in the mood to put up with a lot of innuendo. And she definitely didn't want to find herself daydreaming about the detective's shoulders again.

Before he could say anything, however, one of the officers called Wes from the other side of the room.

"Looks like we've got a message from our perpetrator, Shaw." Standing next to the computer armoire, the cop held a pile of clothes that had been draped over the monitor. Now that the mountain of lace and satin had been moved aside to reveal the screen, the neatly typed words in extra large font were visible from clear across the room.

You're in the wrong business, bitch. Rising, Tempest read the message aloud as she stepped closer to the computer, her frustrations with Wesley Shaw forgotten in the sudden onslaught of cold, clammy fear.

The warning written on her computer screen—the cursor still blinking at the end of the last word—had been left by someone who knew her. The break-in was no random act of city crime, but a calculated plan carried out against her specifically.

The thought made her a little woozy. She'd fought so hard for a small slice of independence in a life filled with commitments to her family's business. The unassuming downtown address and her sculpting gave her a taste of normal life where she wasn't under the constant surveillance of security cameras or family bodyguards. But if her weekend apartment haven wasn't safe, did that mean she'd have to return to the Boucher clan compound that was as secure as Fort Knox and just about as homey?

"Tempest?" Detective Shaw stood beside her now, his voice quieter. Softer, even. But the gaze he directed on her remained detached and—could she be reading him right?—suspicious. "I think it's time we talked more specifically about your line of work."

Tempest chewed her lip, trying to figure out what this man was driving at and why she'd roused his suspicions. Unfortunately, he'd roused a different sort of feeling altogether within her. But no matter what she thought of Detective Wesley Shaw, his brusque manners and undeniable sex appeal, she recognized him as her best hope of keeping her studio a safe retreat.

Somehow she would ignore this unwelcome hum of attraction and do whatever it took to help Wes with his case.

2

"HOW MUCH TIME do you have, Detective?" Tempest wrapped her arms around herself, clearly shaken by the note on her computer screen. "As the temporary CEO of Boucher Enterprises, I'm involved in overseeing many smaller companies in a wide variety of businesses. I also support my studio with my sculpting, so I consider that a line of work as well."

Wes felt a tug of sympathy for her. He'd had enough years in law enforcement to be pretty astute about sizing up people's stories, and Tempest was either a hell of an actress or genuinely surprised and scared to have found her home ransacked.

Of course, that didn't clear her of wrongdoing. She could still be connected to his murder case, or have some hand in the prostitution ring his informant assured him operated under the guise of the MatingGame.com name. Her genuine fear and surprise might simply stem from dismay that someone was on to her.

Hell, for that matter, maybe his sudden eagerness to clear her name had more to do with the fact that he wouldn't mind getting to know her better. Thoughts of her dressed in some of the skimpy lingerie scattered all over the apartment invaded his brain despite his most valiant attempts to staunch them. Was she wearing an outfit like that under her pantsuit right now?

Shoving aside the thought, he forced himself to focus on the case. On her valid worries.

"Do you have reason to believe any of your assorted businesses could be involved in illegal practices?" This was the revealing question, the one that could give her away if she hid an affiliation to a high-priced call girl ring. She certainly had all the right social connections to provide the city's wealthiest men with escorts.

And damned if he didn't really hate that idea.

The mountains of lingerie strewn all over her apartment took on a more sinister meaning.

"Detective Shaw, I assure you if I had any reason to suspect one of my companies engaged in illegal practices, it would already be shut down." She fixed her tawny stare, eyes as cold and remote as the chunk of smoky quartz at her neck. "If you have any grounds for suspecting one of my businesses is involved in something devious, I urge you to fill me in immediately so I can put the proper balls on the chopping block."

The threat seemed all the more convincing in light of the disembodied clay penis he'd unearthed earlier. He hadn't expected so much fervor from a woman he planned to keep on his suspect list.

Did it make him sadistic that Tempest Boucher and her bloodthirsty promise were turning into the most interesting case he'd had in nearly two years?

As the web of intrigue around this mystery tightened, Wes experienced the first hint of enjoyment in
his job that he'd had in far too long. "Is that how
Boucher Enterprises deals with employees who
don't toe the company line?"

"It is while I'm at the helm. My family has been
through enough over the past eight months without
adding the media frenzy any illegal businesses practices would cause."

"Do you keep work-related files on your home
computer?" His gaze strayed back to the PC where
the officer had just finished fingerprinting the keyboard. Wes wanted to get his hands on that computer
to see what secrets he could shake loose from the cir-
cuitry.

Besides, better to think about laying his hands on
the computer than think about using them on the
woman in front of him who needed to be off-limits
for as long as she was a suspect.

"Nothing related to Boucher Enterprises, but I do
the accounting for my sculpting work here." She
snorted. "Such as it is. It's not exactly keeping me
in high style. And now that all my inventory has
been destroyed—"

She broke off, surprising Wes with a hint of
vulnerability he hadn't expected. The woman lived
her life in a relentless public spotlight, ran a company with a net worth that boggled the imagination,
and could afford anything her heart desired. Yet she
seemed genuinely distressed about the loss of her
homemade statues.

"If it's any consolation, insurance ought to cover

their value." Maybe that wasn't what she wanted to hear, but his practical side couldn't help pointing out she wouldn't be hurt financially.

Her curt nod and well-camouflaged sniffle assured him he hadn't consoled her in the least.

"I'm sure you're right. Do you think the person who broke in here was looking for business information of some sort?" She relieved the other officer of his handful of lingerie and the guy got back to work looking around the apartment. Tempest tossed the silky pile of undergarments on the arm of a red floral club chair.

Wes couldn't say how long he stared at the stack of lace and satin, imagining the black silk hugging Tempest's hips, the blue netting cupping generous breasts...

But he knew it took a Herculean effort to pull his thoughts back to reality. Blinking hard, he wrenched his gaze away.

"Possibly." Deciding he was making zero progress by waiting for her to incriminate herself, Wes laid more of his cards on the table, still searching for some telltale reaction. At the very least, by sharing his suspicions he would put her on the defensive if she was guilty. Maybe she'd trip up and give him the lead he needed. "I'm investigating a small company owned by Boucher Enterprises. MatingGame.com?"

"The Internet dating service?"

"You're familiar with the business?"

"I brought them aboard myself shortly before my father's death." She whistled to her dog and absently pet the animal while she spoke. "They had a talented web mistress who keeps the site fresh and provides great visibility all over the Web, but they were being inundated by crank dating résumés and starting to flounder under client dissatisfaction. Boucher brought the financial help they needed to screen all their clients by collecting more information. I believe they're turning a very healthy profit now."

"*I* believe they are a front for a prostitution ring." He kept his gaze direct. Detached. That was a crucial part of interrogation unless you had a damn good reason for wanting your suspect to think you were on their side.

Wes didn't know whether he'd struck pay dirt or if he'd merely scared the hell out of her, but she swayed on her feet at the news.

Damn.

"Are you okay?" He reached for her on instinct, pushing aside his need to dig for the truth long enough to steady her.

His hand went automatically to her waist, securing her at the base of her spine. Right away he knew touching her had been a mistake, but what the hell else could he have done? She looked as though she'd seen a damn ghost.

Too bad all he could think of was how tiny her waist felt under her jacket. The tailored cut wasn't nearly tailored enough, the fabric not doing justice to the cinch of her midsection between gently flared hips and incredible cleavage.

Her scent—something rich and warm that made him think of the hot chestnuts sold by street vendors all winter—made him feel damn light-headed too. Good thing he would let her go any second now.

Yup. Any minute.

"I'm fine." Tempest cleared her throat, the soft vibration of her voice reverberating gently against his palm where he still touched her. She stepped away before he remembered he was supposed to be letting go.

Cursing himself and his stupid sex-starved senses, Wes regretted the loss of mental control. He hadn't done anything outwardly inappropriate, but his thoughts were another story. Worst of all, he'd lost track of his instincts since they'd gotten mixed with lust.

Where the hell was the cop buzz when he needed it? It seemed to have been soundly thrashed by a much louder hum of desire.

"I don't know anything about MatingGame being involved in illegal activity, but you caught me off guard since—" She peered over her shoulder toward the other officers in the apartment. "Can we possibly speak in private?"

Surprised at her apparent need to confess, Wes couldn't deny a rush of disappointment. The sexual hunger simmering in his veins had been really rooting for this woman's innocence.

"Sure." He shouted to the cops finishing up their routine search for evidence and quickly cleared the room of everyone but the two of them and Eloise, who curled up in front of the door for a snooze.

Wes hoped Vanessa wouldn't show up on the scene too soon now that Tempest appeared so close to telling him what she knew. His partner had planned to investigate a few other leads on their murder case, but he expected she'd arrive at the precinct soon.

Now he settled in the club chair, a safe distance from the temptation presented by the first woman to send sparks his way in too long.

And didn't it just figure she was going to turn out to be part of a prostitution ring?

Tempest eyed the muscular cop sprawled in a chair two sizes too small for him and prayed she was making the right decision by trusting him. But if he was investigating MatingGame, he might as well know everything she knew.

She sank down into the couch across from him and dug out the old memories that had caused her family so much pain.

"You're probably familiar with the scandal surrounding my father's death last year while he was in Mexico?" It had been the subject of speculation in the papers for weeks, making it nearly impossible to grieve privately.

"Heart attack during sex with a much younger lover, right?" Detective Shaw didn't look scandalized in the least. Somehow, that made it easier to continue.

"Most people assumed it was a heart attack, allowing us to keep quiet the fact that the Mexican officials said he actually died of asphyxiation. You know how some people think cutting off their oxygen supply will increase the power of their release?" She waited for his nod, her cheeks heating at the nature of the discussion. She'd never been a shy woman, but the frank sex talk unnerved her.

Especially in light of her inconvenient attraction to the cop.

"He died during kinky sex?" One eyebrow lifted.

"Yes. And the woman involved might have come under more scrutiny if my mother hadn't assured police my father had been perfecting ways to achieve the ultimate release throughout their marriage. It was one of the core reasons my parents fought." Her mother had been horrified by her husband's increasing obsession with pushing sex to the limit, finally walking out when he'd nearly strangled himself, although they'd never actually divorced. Apparently Ray Boucher demanded as much from his sexual encounters as he had from every other facet of his glittering, over-the-top lifestyle. "And as it happened, the woman my father had been with that last night wasn't really a girlfriend. She was a one-night stand he'd met through MatingGame."

Wes sat straighter in his chair, his long, lean body suddenly charged with alertness. "She never said anything to the press?"

"My mother and I made a trip south of the border to appeal to her sense of common decency and asked her to keep the sordid details to herself since the local officials didn't leak the information to the media." The woman had been nice enough and she'd been as eager as they were to put the ordeal behind her. "We helped her to relocate overseas so she wouldn't be faced with the situation day in and day out over the turbulent months that followed."

"You paid her off?"

"Hardly. She was down on her luck after a divorce left her broke, which was why my mother and I thought it would be just as well to help her start over again. Last I heard, she'd learned to speak Italian and settled just outside of Florence."

"But you felt guilty enough about the whole situation to confess all this to me," he pointed out with a bluntness Tempest began to recognize as part of his investigative style.

Or maybe it was just his personality. She had found it rather cold at first, but after a lifetime surrounded by people who were often pleasant to her face only for personal gain, she was beginning to find his direct manner more appealing.

Or maybe it was simply all those hard male muscles she found interesting. She hadn't been enticed to get close to a man in a very long time.

"I don't feel guilty about it in the least since no one outside his family needs to know what happened to my father. I was just taken aback when you mentioned MatingGame could be a cover for a prostitution ring." She had thought the scandal of having her father die in bed while having adulterous sex with a woman half his age had been bad. Imagine the repercussions if the adulterous sex turned out to be part of an encounter with a prostitute?

The tabloids would have a field day, her mother would be humiliated and Boucher Enterprises would suffer. And while Tempest and her family were well-insulated from the rises and falls of the business, she couldn't help but think of the people who worked for the company in one capacity or another. *Those* were the people who would suffer the most.

"You're worried about the negative press that will ensue if people learn your father cavorted with a prostitute." Shaw nodded knowingly, as if that statement summed up the situation.

"It's a lot more complicated than that." Tension built in her forehead, the sure sign of another stress headache coming on. She could have handled all this better if she'd at least had her weekly dose of *Days of Our Lives*. Damn it, melodrama like this belonged on her television screen, not in her living room. "You know how many people depend on our company for their livelihood? Those are the people who get hurt when my family comes under attack.

"My mother will console herself with shopping. My late father's board of directors will unload their stock options and jump on early retirement. But what about the thousands of people we employ around the globe? They don't deserve to lose their jobs because my father suffered a midlife crisis from the time he turned thirty until the day he died."

Levering herself off the couch, Tempest stepped over the piles of rubble from the break-in, slowly making her way toward the kitchen where a bottle of Tylenol waited.

"What about you?" The cool-as-you-please detective merely followed her with his eyes, though his long limbs retained their alert stance, as if ready to pounce at any moment. "What would you do if Boucher Enterprises takes a financial nosedive?"

The question made her head throb all the more.

Fishing through a maze of cooking spices and boxes of Milk-Bones in every conceivable flavor, she found the pain reliever and popped two in her mouth. Downing them with a cold glass of water, she took deep breaths and reminded herself nothing catastrophic had happened to the company yet. She could still fix this.

"I'll admit it makes things harder for me. As temporary CEO, I'm eager to unload my job and it will make the position less attractive if the company is struggling."

All the more reason to address the matter of MatingGame before the problem exploded underneath her. "In fact," she continued, a plan slowly taking shape, "if MatingGame is a front for something sordid, I can have it shut down in a matter of minutes."

Infused with new energy now that she had a strategy, she moved to find the phone, which no longer rested in its usual place on the kitchen counter.

"No." Detective Shaw rose from his seat and was in her face in no time. He moved with a swiftness that surprised her.

"What do you mean, 'no'?" Her breath caught at their sudden proximity, his tall, lanky frame close enough to touch.

Not that she would allow herself the pleasure. She'd been far too aware of him ever since he'd touched her earlier, as if her body had captured that quick impression of his hand on her back and had been seeking to recreate the moment ever since. Ridiculous, maybe. But sort of intriguing considering she hadn't been even remotely interested in any man over the last months of nose-to-the-grindstone work.

What was it about the plainspoken police detective that turned her head and made her—she fidgeted to admit it, even to herself—*horny?* She'd never been the type to get all keyed up over a guy. Why him? Why now?

The timing for her sudden bout of lust surely sucked.

"I don't have the evidence I need to prove Mating-Game is a shady business." He had oddly precise articulation for a man who'd probably seen the seamiest underbelly of the city. Glaring down at her from his height, which would have dwarfed her even if she hadn't been wearing her running shoes, Wesley Shaw was warning her in no uncertain terms.

Too bad he was also turning her on—big-time. Her breath hitched in her throat as she envisioned having her way with such a big, powerful man. She'd overcome a lot of personal insecurities in the past year, but she'd never had the chance to test her sexual confidence.

This was *so* the wrong time.

"It would better suit my company to pull the rug out from under them, Detective." Folding her arms across her chest, she glared right back, hoping like hell she wasn't giving out any "do-me" vibe to mirror her sexually charged thoughts. "I don't need any evidence to withdraw my support immediately. I won't allow Boucher Enterprises to be dragged through the mud just so you can make your case."

They stood too close together but Tempest wasn't about to back down now. She hadn't gleaned many of her father's killer instincts when it came to business, but she knew enough about body language to comprehend she didn't dare give this man any ground now.

Of course, there was a whole other dynamic to their body language that didn't have a damn thing to do with prostitution, MatingGame, Boucher Enterprises or even her ransacked apartment.

"I don't care about busting prostitutes." He lowered his voice to a pitch that seemed just right for how close their bodies loomed and all wrong for a detached, intelligent conversation between strangers.

"You don't?" Tempest cringed inwardly to hear her own voice hit a soft note. What was she thinking to engage in guy-girl games with the cop investigating a break-in?

Bad, bad idea.

"No. I'm trying to catch the murderer masquerading as a prostitute."

His words reverberated in her ears, his point resonating until the meaning loomed large and ugly just outside the kitchenette area of her apartment. She blinked hard to gather her bearings, but when she opened her eyes her world still seemed slightly off-kilter and her stress headache now pounded to the forefront of her brain.

Body language be damned, she needed breathing room.

"I think I'd better sit down." Tempest sidled past him, attempting to get her bearings away from the confusing heat that flared between them. She stepped on a piece of statuary, the broken clay crushing into dust on the hardwood floor beneath her sneaker.

"I need your help, Tempest." He was right behind her, following her toward the sofa.

Her apartment seemed to shrink with him in it, his presence big and male and dominating her scrambled thoughts.

"I don't know how I can help you, Detective, and I sure don't understand how having my apartment broken into relates to murder." She paused beside the sofa, unwilling to take a seat if it meant this man would insinuate himself beside her. She couldn't think with him so close.

"You can help me." His gray eyes seemed so confident. So certain. "And you can start by calling me Wes."

"I don't think that's such a good idea." She needed barriers to ward off the train wreck certain to ensue if she ever acted on her newfound lust for one of New York's finest.

She dated artists. Men who weren't afraid to explore their creative side, or at very least, their sensitive side. Wesley—Wes—didn't look like the type to get in touch with his emotions anytime soon.

"It's an excellent idea because you and I are going to get to know each other a hell of a lot better for the next few days—weeks—however long it takes for me to catch my bad guy." He frowned. "Or bad *girl* in this case."

"That's impossible." No way, no how, would she

allow herself to get any closer to this man. She'd already experienced the sizzle of his briefest touch. How could she ward off that kind of sexual firepower for days—possibly weeks—on end? "I've got a multimillion dollar company to run. A CEO to hire. Do you have any idea how much my father's death has compromised his business and all the people who count on Boucher to make their living?"

"No. But I have a fair idea that your earnings will continue to go down once it's made public that the Boucher heiress can't make time in her busy schedule to help police catch a killer."

His words delivered a resounding slap to her conscience, a plea she couldn't very well deny. No matter that her life had been turned upside down, or that her bid for independence from her powerful family would be put on hold until she could recreate her inventory of artworks. She needed to pull her head out of her own problems and remind her body that Wes Shaw was off-limits long enough to help him find his criminal.

She was so caught up in her own thoughts, she didn't realize Wes reached for her until his hands were on her upper arms, the fabric of her crimson jacket practically incinerating beneath that simple touch.

"Please, Tempest." His gray gaze jump-started an erratic and totally juvenile beating of her heart. "Help me."

She was in over her head with this man after knowing him for less than two hours. But he needed her help and she planned to give it to him, consequences be damned. And not just because she found herself thinking about what it might be like to kiss that blunt mouth of his.

No, Tempest planned to help him because she wouldn't allow her personal space, her private creative haven, to be invaded by street thieves, or prostitutes, or—she took a steeling breath—*murderers.*

Yet, even as she gave him an affirmative nod, she kept hearing a familiar swell of music somewhere in the back of her mind.

Like sand through the hourglass…

In the course of a couple of hours, Tempest's life had definitely become a soap opera.

3

OVER THE NEXT HOUR, Wes helped Tempest sort through the wreckage of her apartment. Cleanup wasn't a part of the NYPD response to a break-in, but as a detective and a nine-year veteran on the force, he'd bought himself a little leeway when it came to handling cases.

He used the time to phone his partner, dodging most of Vanessa's questions since he didn't want to discuss the case where Tempest might hear. There would be time enough to catch up with Vanessa tomorrow. For tonight, as long as he had won Tempest's compliance, he planned to find out everything he could about MatingGame and her role in the Internet dating service.

Now, he taped up another box of broken statuary pieces while she swept up some of the dust. She'd changed into a pair of jeans and a simple black blouse at some point, probably while he'd been on the phone. The velvet choker with the smoky crystal remained around her neck, but she'd tied back her curly dark hair with a black and red zebra-print bandana.

He stacked the third box of smashed clay pieces

on top of the others and then paused to watch her while she worked. She wasn't at all what he'd expected.

His mental image of a Manhattan socialite pretty much coincided with the stereotype—vain, spoiled, self-involved. Yet here she was, living in a Chelsea studio that had to be far beneath her financial means, with no household help in sight. She swept up her own messes, microwaved her own popcorn and kept stealing glances at a small television that seemed to be tuned nonstop to overblown daytime dramas. Even without the audio, the action on screen snagged most of her attention while she cleaned.

Except for the handful of times he'd caught her sneaking glances at him. Some kind of heat sparked between them and Wes would be stupid to deny it. He didn't plan to act on it—in fact, he would make damn sure to ignore it—but the sexual friction had made for a tense day. He was pretty sure she fought against the chemistry even harder than him.

"Do you mind if I have a look through your computer?" Wes propped his elbow on the stack of boxes and studied her. "Ever since we found the note from the perpetrator, I've been curious to take a look around your files and see if he left a trail." Besides, staring at a computer screen would prevent him from staring at Tempest.

"Sure." Setting the broom aside she washed her hands and pulled two bowls out of a cabinet. "We can have our dinner—such as it is—while we surf. Maybe then you can explain to me what Mating-Game has to do with your murder case." She pulled two bottles of water out of the refrigerator. "Is water okay? The secret to my latest diet is not to bring anything in the house that I shouldn't eat."

Wes grabbed the bottles from her and carried them toward the computer, grateful for another topic. "I thought you were going to prove me wrong about jet-setting heiresses."

"I'm not a jet-setting heiress so I'm proving you wrong already." Her voice followed him a few steps behind as the scent of buttered popcorn filled the room.

Eloise lifted her head from her paws as he walked by her, tail thumping the floor.

"You're living on a diet of popcorn and water." He slid into the red, high-backed chair in front of the computer and told himself that finding out more about Tempest was part of his job. The fact that he happened to be enjoying himself was a bonus. "You must know that's exactly what I'd expect from you highbrow types. You probably had a half ounce of cottage cheese on a lettuce leaf for lunch, right?"

"Wrong again." She set down their popcorn on a foldout shelf before pulling over one of the dining room chairs to sit beside him. Before she lowered herself into the chair, she whistled to Eloise and tossed the dog a pink Milk-Bone.

"I bet I'm not far off." Wes concentrated on the scent of popcorn in an effort to shut out the soft fragrance of the woman making herself comfortable next to him.

She sure didn't seem like the prostitution type, even with the high percentage of lacy undergarments still strewn around her apartment like visual sex triggers guaranteed to make him start drooling. And she didn't seem to be hiding anything, either. Other than her lunch menu, of course.

"I skipped lunch actually," she finally admitted, her gaze fixed on the computer screen as he pulled up the "Properties" information box on the unnamed document informing Tempest she was in the wrong business.

"Even worse than a lettuce leaf." He tossed a handful of popcorn in his mouth and jotted down the time the document had been created. 12:53 pm. "You said you got home around two?"

"I got to the building at five minutes before two. My meeting ran late today and then Eloise stopped to beg the hot pretzel vendor for a treat." She glared at Eloise who sniffed the floor for any leftover crumbs.

"It's no wonder your dog has to beg on the street if you feed her like you feed yourself." He cracked open his bottle of water and took a swig before digging into the popcorn bowl again. "But it's a damn good thing you didn't get here any sooner today since you missed your uninvited guest by less than an hour."

Wes didn't want to think about how different his day would have been if he'd been called to Tempest's apartment on an assault case. Or worse.

His popcorn stuck in his throat.

"Tell me why you think MatingGame is involved in prostitution." Tempest tucked her feet underneath her thighs, folding herself up into a more comfortable position on her chair.

Not that he'd let his gaze wander over her delectable body. He was simply making smart cop observations.

Yeah, that was it.

"Anonymous tip." He clicked through a few more screens before opening her browser and surfing to the MatingGame site. "Add that to the fact that our murder victim had a reputation for visiting prostitutes every Saturday night, and then this past Saturday his appointment book had an entry to meet someone he designated simply as a blonde from MatingGame."

She wriggled in her seat beside him, the wooden dining room chair squeaking as she moved.

"Maybe he got tired of paying for sex and decided to use a more tried and true means of getting horizontal." She reached over him to point out a little red box at the bottom of the MatingGame home page. "Click here to move straight to the dating profiles."

"I don't get paid to come up with the most creative scenarios for a crime. I follow the obvious path first." Wes took a deep breath to steel himself against the surge of hunger brought on by the soft shift of her body beside his. She was close enough that he could hear the whisper of fabric as she moved. Her shoulder brushed his arm as she leaned in front of him, and he could have sworn one wayward curl of her dark hair skimmed his cheek.

Of course, the breath that he hoped would steel his nerves only filled his nostrils with her warm, nutty scent—something sultry and feminine and definitely edible. Whatever it was, he damn well wanted a taste.

He clicked the red box she'd indicated with a vengeance, hoping like hell she wouldn't have any reason to point to the computer screen again. How could a man keep his mind on work with such an abundance of soft femininity leaning and bending and stretching beside him?

"Are you comfortable yet?" He turned on her, not meaning to glare, but didn't she realize how distracting all that wriggling could be?

"You got the good chair." Frowning, she looped an arm over the back of the wooden seat. "I can't sit still if I'm not comfy."

Damnation. He stood, silently rolling the red office chair toward her until she swapped places with him. He dragged the wooden chair in front of the computer and turned it around so he could straddle the seat. They would both be better off if he didn't get too relaxed in her living room anyhow.

"So the obvious answer is that his MatingGame date was a prostitute?" She reached over him again to tap the blank screen with one manicured finger. "I think the women's profiles are on the left. Sorry my dial-up connection is slow, but you can go ahead and click here and it will advance you to the next screen."

This wasn't going to work. Wes was choking on his own lust. The women he'd slept with in the last eighteen months hadn't been people he'd pursued. They'd shown interest in him, he'd succumbed to biology. The encounters had been simple. Neat. Easy.

And completely unlike the heat licking over him because of one curvy, wriggly, delicious-smelling woman. It would be different if he could just take her right now and get it over with. Right there, in her red chair, where she'd damn well be comfortable.

Only she wouldn't stay comfortable for long. If he had his way, she'd be sighing, moaning and writhing all over him until she'd achieved body-rocking sexual bliss.

While they waited for the page to load on the screen, Wes downed the rest of his bottle of water but didn't come close to dousing the heat inspired by Tempest Boucher.

"There we go," she murmured as thumbnail photos of dozens of women appeared on the monitor. "I haven't looked at the site in quite a while, but if I remember correctly, these are the dating profiles for every woman in the system except for the clients who sign up for the Blind Date service. When we took over the company, we helped MatingGame make sure all the e-mail addresses were verified to cut down on bogus profiles. I can't imagine women who were prostituting themselves would give out information where they could be tracked."

"You'd be surprised." Forcing himself to concentrate on his case, Wes enlarged two of the profiles for closer inspection. "The city has slacked off on prosecuting crimes some people argue are victimless. Because of the lack of vigilance, escort services thrive and they can be very aggressive about advertising."

She frowned. "I've never studied the site that thoroughly from anything but a business point of view, but I know firsthand that valid relationships have formed through the help of MatingGame. One of the company accountants got married last fall to a guy she met through the service."

"Probably most of it is legit. My guess is that there's a protected link, some hidden branch of the business that hires out escorts." He scanned the profiles he'd pulled, not really sure what he was looking for. His professional hunger to solve the mystery seemed to be slowly giving way to a different kind of hunger that wouldn't do either of them any good.

"Preferences—threesomes, foursomes and more." Tempest read aloud one of the entries in the provocative profiles designed to generate plenty of interest for people looking for a date. She sounded vaguely scandalized, but that didn't stop her from reaching for the mouse once again. "Do you think she'll just pick one guy or will she choose four and ask them all to meet her at once?"

"Wait." Wes restrained her wrist, unable to sit still while she stretched her delectable body in front of him for the third time. "I'll get it."

She froze there, body unmoving, her pulse pounding beneath the slight pressure of his thumb. "I just wanted to see what came up when you clicked on the hyperlink for threesomes. I guess I didn't realize people were so…*specific* about what they wanted in a partner."

"But if we start following all the options that catch our attention we'll be here all night." He held her wrist, held her gaze, hoping all the while she'd comprehend his real meaning.

It would have required a supreme act of willpower not to skim his thumb over the silky skin. And after wrestling his growing attraction to Tempest over the last few hours, Wes found he no longer possessed the restraint. He traced a line down the delicate tendons there, absorbing the smooth perfection of her.

Her lips parted, her faded lipstick revealing the natural color of her soft pink mouth beneath. Hypnotized by the perfect shape of the lush Cupid's bow, Wes hovered closer until Tempest pulled away.

"Then I guess we'd better keep our attention more strictly focused." Freeing her wrist, she reached for her water bottle and unscrewed the top. "I'll check out the threesomes later."

Wes wanted to redirect his thoughts but couldn't seem to force himself to turn back to the computer. Lust still surged through him like the Eighth Avenue Express and she just shrugged it aside, as if it was all in a day's work for a pampered, privileged heiress. Did she get off on making men drool and then leaving them wanting?

He didn't know what games this woman was playing, but he damn well wouldn't be leaving her apartment until he found out.

AS SHE STARED BACK into the stormiest gray eyes she'd ever seen, Tempest decided Wes looked angry. No, more like quietly seething.

Well—newsflash—she wasn't exactly thrilled to

have him waltz in here and take over her home, her computer and her hormones, either.

"Seems to me you've made concentration impossible." Wes shoved aside their popcorn bowls before taking her water bottle from her hand, carefully screwing on the top, and pushing that away, too. "Has it ever occurred to you all that stretching and reaching over me combined with your infernal fascination with threesomes just might distract a man?"

"I am not fascinated by—" How dare he? Of all the presumptuous, arrogant things to insinuate. "Are you accusing me of flirting with you?"

"What would you call it?" He didn't raise his voice, instead keeping his tone very, very soft. "I'm not opposed to starting something between us if the appropriate time arises after I close my case. But I'll be damned if I'll let you get away with a lot of suggestive talk and sidling up close only to have you leave me high and dry and completely incapable of getting any work done."

"You think I'm playing the tease?" And didn't that just beat all? "I was nice enough to make you popcorn and I didn't even say a word when you took over my computer keys like you own them, even though I'm more familiar with my computer and this Web site than you are. Can I help it if I'm a little impatient to get through our work for the night so I can clean up the rest of the apartment and get back to my life?"

"But not impatient enough to point out the threesomes link?" He eased back ever so slightly, his self-assured body language somehow conveying a smugness that he'd made his point.

"So sue me for a prurient streak." She had *so* not been flirting with him.

Had she?

Forcing herself to consider the notion, she wondered if her sexual impulses could conspire to act without her explicit permission? What if her artistic persona and businesswoman facade hid yet another facet—a decadent and determined inner seductress? She'd blossomed into a daytime TV heroine in record time today. All she needed was a bout with amnesia.

Maybe she had fallen through the damn sand in the hourglass at 2:00 p.m. today. Instead of transitioning from businesswoman Tempest to artist Tempest this afternoon as usual, she'd walked into a time fugue and ended up in the middle of the drama.

Frustrated with herself, with him and with the undeniable attraction she felt for a man she probably had nothing in common with, she forged ahead. "Look, I'm sorry if it seemed like I was coming on to you. The profiles happened to intrigue me."

"So you're saying your sudden interest in threesomes didn't have a damn thing to do with me?"

"Correct."

He grinned. A slow, sexy, I'm-going-to-have-you grin that incited a sensual shiver down her spine. "Good. Because I'm not the kind of guy who shares."

TEMPEST was still recovering from that grin two hours later as Wes clicked through profile after profile, searching for some clue on his murder case.

She might have been able to forget about their exchange if she hadn't been subjected to reading through all sorts of kinky sexual fetishes and fantasy requirements for every woman in search of a date on the MatingGame site. But honestly, how could she think about motive and intent when every page that scrolled over her screen referenced a new sex act she'd never tried?

She was beginning to feel very deprived and inexperienced, but she had no intention of allowing Wes to read any hint of hunger in her eyes. Restless and on edge, she sprang up from her chair.

"I should take Eloise for a walk." Seizing on the idea like a lifeline, she started picking up their popcorn dishes along with some Thai food take-out containers from the dinner Wes insisted they eat.

"I'll go with you." He unfolded his tall body from the unforgiving wooden chair that had to be damn uncomfortable by now.

"That's okay. You finish up and I'll be back in a minute." Maybe then she could reclaim her apartment and her wayward sexual thoughts.

"And what if your apartment is being watched?" He took the empty containers from her arms and dumped them in the wastebasket they'd left in the middle of the studio during their clean-up efforts. "If my murder case is linked to your break-in, then you're dealing with a dangerous threat. My guess is the killer came here hoping to erase her profile from the MatingGame database and when she didn't find the Web site files on the computer, she trashed the apartment and left the message to scare you."

If Tempest hadn't been frightened before, she sure as hell was starting to worry now. Almost enough to pack up her stuff and sleep at her family's ostentatious place on Park Avenue, but not quite. "Don't you think this murdering prostitute chick was a little excessive in wrecking the apartment? She broke every statue I ever made."

"Don't forget we're dealing with a criminal mind. Studies show a high percentage of these people are mentally unbalanced in one way or another." He whistled to Eloise, who came bounding over, pink tongue lolling out one side of her mouth. "All the more reason to let me go with you tonight."

"You haven't seen Eloise in action." She couldn't let Wes start thinking he needed to look out for her. She hadn't even managed to free herself from her family business yet, so she definitely couldn't afford to get mixed up with anybody who might start having expectations of her. "She might look sweet and friendly, but she's as kick-ass as any police dog when it comes to watching my back. I couldn't ask for better protection."

"Unless the killer shoots her." Wes pulled Eloise's leash down from a hook by the front door like he'd been living there all his life. "I'm not trying to scare you, Tempest, but you owe it to yourself and your dog to be careful until I catch this person."

She willed herself to nod her head. He was right, and she knew it.

Tempest just hadn't figured out how to reconcile her need for independence with her desire to stay alive. The choice might not have been so difficult except that she wanted to stand on her own two feet and Wes Shaw looked like a man well-versed in sweeping women right off them.

4

WES STUMBLED over his own feet the next morning, bleary-eyed and fuzzyheaded after too little sleep. Blindly he fought his way through the maze of gym equipment that accounted for the sum total of his living room furnishings. Despite his best efforts, he stubbed his toe on a dumbbell and unleashed a string of curses that brought his St. Bernard, Kong, running from the bedroom with a woof.

"All clear," Wes shouted to the dog whose protective instincts would have made Miss Independent Boucher break out in hives.

She'd practically hyperventilated the night before when Wes suggested he spend the night at her place for safety reasons. Suddenly, she'd developed all sorts of plans for beefing up the security around her apartment, insisting she'd be fine without his help. He'd tried to convince her to go back to her family's place where she apparently stayed during the week, but she'd been stubborn on that count, too.

Damned independent woman. Thinking of her there alone had cost him plenty of shut-eye.

He'd stayed up half the night thinking about her,

after checking and re-checking every lock in her apartment. Her door had shown no visible signs of tampering, but the only way into the third floor space had been through the front entrance or the door to the fire escape, which had a dead bolt whose lock was collecting dust. Wes had talked to her superintendent along with the old woman who lived a few doors down and had been home during the break-in. Neither of them had heard or seen anything unusual.

After forcing himself to leave her building, he'd gone back to the precinct to go over his case file on the murder and enter an incident report about Tempest's intruder. But late-night brainstorming with Vanessa hadn't helped them figure out the connections between their murder investigation and Tempest or MatingGame.

At least they'd eliminated Tempest as a murder suspect since she had an ironclad alibi for the victim's time of death. A lady photographer caught her date with a local coffee shop owner on film for a tabloid column, and Wes ended up with the distinct displeasure of confirming with the guy that he and Tempest had taken in a movie together that night. Too bad no amount of the man's assurances that they were just friends did a damn thing to improve Wes's mood. Obviously, he shouldn't care who she dated, but it irritated him to picture her with the artsy-fartsy coffee shop guy who managed to weave Kafka references into conversation on two separate occasions.

And as if that wasn't bad enough, Wes now discovered he'd lost his taste for coffee.

Reaching into the refrigerator for a bottle of some

bogus energy drink, he chugged a few swigs and started thinking through his day. First and foremost was making a phone call to authorities in Mexico for some more information on Tempest's father. Not that he didn't trust foreign cops—he just didn't trust *any* cop outside his own precinct.

A suspicious nature came with the badge. And Wes had all the more reason to be careful with Tempest since his instincts couldn't be trusted where she was concerned. He planned to check her out ten ways to Sunday so the next time he showed up on her doorstep, he wouldn't have to hold himself back from the attraction that had gnawed at him ever since he'd first walked into her apartment.

Because the next time she leaned and stretched or wriggled those oh-so-fine curves of hers in his direction, he had every intention of showing her how appreciative he could be.

TEMPEST DIDN'T APPRECIATE the stomach-clenching fear her intruder had instilled in her.

She might have given in to her worries and spent the weekend at the Boucher family home if it hadn't been for Eloise. Her dog had slept by her all night, ready to keep away any returning criminals or stray bogeymen who threatened her safe haven. Too bad her faithful canine wasn't as effective at keeping away men who threatened her peace of mind.

This morning, Tempest had been awake since dawn, cleaning and organizing the studio until she'd achieved some semblance of its former order. Now she reviewed the summary of her missed *Days* episode online while she told herself she wasn't listening for Wes's footsteps in the hallway.

She'd read the same line three times about the latest character to come back from the dead—normally a topic she loved—when Eloise ran to the door and barked.

Tempest peered through the peephole in time to spy a familiar figure striding down the hall. Obviously, her dog was even better attuned to the new man in their lives than Tempest. By the time Wes rapped on the door, she was already opening it.

"Did you even check to make sure it was me?" Wes frowned at her, his vintage suit replaced by faded jeans and a blue T-shirt underneath a long tweed wool coat.

In a word—*yum.* The more fitted clothes were put to good use on a man as ruthlessly toned as Wes Shaw.

"Eloise told me it was you." She opened the door wider, her gaze flicking south as he walked past her into the apartment.

So she noticed he had a great butt, okay? That didn't mean she was going to do anything about it. Slamming the door shut behind him, she braced herself for another round of temptation. She'd already decided today would be all about clearing her name with Wes and helping him find out what was going on with MatingGame.

"She *told* you?" He leaned down to pet her pooch's ears before tossing a folder on the boxes of debris she'd stacked by the front door. "Lucky for you, I own a dog, too, or I might think you were losing your mind."

"You have a dog?" She shouldn't ask him about it, didn't need any reason to like this guy any more than she already did, but curiosity got the better of her.

"Kong. She's been with me since— For about two years."

She sensed more to that story, but it didn't look like he'd be sharing any more of it since he backed closer to her computer.

"Kong's a girl?"

"Trust me, it fits. She's not a girlie girl." He bent over her keyboard and scanned a few lines about her soap opera before moving his hand to the escape key. "You mind if we pick up where we left off last night?"

Her heart slugged in her chest at the images that idea conjured. What if they picked up right at the point when Wes had been sitting beside her, his steely gray gaze drifting down over her mouth? Lingering.

She blinked hard, waiting for her clearheaded thoughts to return. Daydreaming about Wes wouldn't get anything accomplished today and she refused to let a little sexual attraction delay his progress on clearing her business's name.

"That's fine. I placed a call to the MatingGame head Web mistress who still oversees the day-to-day operations of the company. She's out of town until Wednesday, but I left her an urgent message that we needed to discuss the business. I can't imagine MatingGame is involved in anything improper, but if there is trouble in the company, this woman will know exactly where to look for it."

"Good. Were you able to access her files for the site?" Wes slid into the seat in front of the computer and clicked a few buttons to review recently down-loaded material.

"Her assistant sent a disk over by courier. It's in the drive now." Tempest watched him go to work on the files, his computer savvy obvious as he opened windows and accessed files.

"Can I get you some coffee?" She could do that much at least, since she would have offered the same to any other visitor.

He grumbled something unintelligible under his breath and then asked for tea.

Three hours and numerous cups of tea later, Wes hadn't found anything unusual in the computer files. He'd forwarded names and addresses to his police station, checking out the women—and even some of the men—who posted profiles on MatingGame. So far not a single person had been linked to prostitu-tion or violent crime. He'd flagged two sex offend-ers who had snuck through the screening process, however, and reported them to police stations in Cal-ifornia and Wisconsin where the profiles originated.

Tempest couldn't help but admire his thorough approach to his work and the noble intentions behind it. She could appreciate the importance of his job, even if it put her on the defensive as owner of the dat-ing company.

Sipping from a small glass of orange juice, she stole past the small desk for the tenth time in the last few hours, curious about his work but not wanting to get too close to him. He'd warned her about sitting beside him last night and she'd taken him at his word. No way would she send him any signals that implied sexual interest.

Even if she felt it.

"If you told me what you were looking for, maybe I could help you find it." She set down her juice to wave her laptop in front of him. "I could work at the table and review files from there."

But Wes scarcely seemed to hear her, his concentration devoted to the text onscreen, which he'd enlarged. "Take a look at this."

She started to lean over his shoulder and then decided she'd be better off just pulling up a chair, since he seemed engrossed in his work anyway. Settling next to him, she retrieved her juice in an effort to keep cool around the sexy detective. "It's the coding for one of the profiles, right?"

Her gaze scanned along the text that suggested the woman who'd written it was especially adept at blow jobs.

Tempest nearly spewed her orange juice.

"Yes. But it's unusual coding since it includes this graphic of an asterisk here and I can't see any explanation on the site for what significance an asterisk has. Do you know?"

Blinking her way past the shock of *blow jobs* written in sixteen-point font, Tempest tried to focus on his question and not wonder if there was actually a technique to good blow jobs. What other key pieces of sex advice had she been missing out on all her adult life?

"I don't know what the asterisk means. Perhaps

it only has significance to the site managers?" She congratulated herself on her calm, intelligent words despite her ridiculous thoughts. "Maybe it means the woman in question is a repeat customer or received a good rating from her dates or something."

"But why put it there unless the Web site wants customers to see it?" Wes turned toward her, swiveling in his chair until he faced her head-on.

"Valid point." She half wondered if the asterisk denoted adept blow job givers. "I can put in another call to the MatingGame people and see what they say."

"What if it denotes the prostitutes in the crowd so that visitors who are aware they're available can make sure they choose from the right pool of women?"

"I don't know." Shrugging, she found it hard to believe MatingGame had anything to do with prostitution. Or was it just that she couldn't bear for her business instincts to have been so dead wrong? "Did you check out other women who have the asterisk graphic on their page?"

"I'll put someone on it. I know you don't want one of your companies to be found guilty of trafficking in sex, but one way or another, I have to get to the bottom of it."

"I'm just as eager as you are to figure out what's going on." She didn't need her board of directors questioning her business decisions now.

Reaching down to the floor, she picked up her laptop to show him how helpful she could be in his case.

Except that her arm brushed his leg as she moved.

JUST AN ACCIDENT?

Wes might have written off the barely-there touch as unintentional, except that coincidences were piling up as fast as he could count them in this investigation. His murder case just happened to be linked to Tempest Boucher, who seemed to be the target of an intruder bent on destruction. And he still wasn't comfortable with the fact that her father had died while out with a MatingGame client, same as the victim in Wes's case.

Maybe the incidents didn't have a damn thing to do with one another and it had all just been chance. But—more likely—the events were genuinely related. He was anxious to speak to the day-to-day operations manager of MatingGame to see if she was selling more than dating advice.

Either way, Wes had reached his personal coincidence quota today. Since Tempest had touched him, he could only believe that she'd meant it.

Shifting beside him, she hefted her small computer onto the desk, her cheeks flushing pink.

"Sorry." She murmured an apology before cracking open the case of her laptop.

"Are you?" He studied her while she flicked through the opening screens as her computer warmed up. One brown curl grazed her temple while the rest remained knotted haphazardly at the back of her head with only a felt tip pen to keep it in place.

She blew the curl away from her eyes impatiently as she huffed out a sigh. "No, actually, I'm not a bit sorry. I can't help you unless I can access the MatingGame site. It's not my fault your he-man sprawl of legs takes up every square foot of space beneath the desk."

He watched her brow furrow in concentration, her lips pursed while she tapped more keys on the laptop. His gaze lingered on her mouth, which appeared deliciously free of lipstick today.

No doubt about it, he wanted her. Her alibi checked out for his case, so he wasn't worried about the ethics of the situation. And although he wanted to find the homicidal hooker who had taken down her victim a week ago, Wes didn't really have any other professional interest in MatingGame. If some facet of the company was involved in prostitution, Wes would stake his reputation that Tempest Boucher didn't know a damn thing about it. Either way, that wasn't his department. Another cop would make that bust, not him.

From where he was sitting, there wasn't a reason in the world not to pursue the only woman to capture his interest in longer than he cared to remember.

"I checked your alibi." He tossed the comment out there, as he navigated his way through a few more profiles of New York–based singles on the MatingGame site.

"Alibi?" Her computer keys stopped tapping.

"For last Saturday night." His gaze wandered over another curly-headed brunette on-screen but the vampish female whose profile touted her S and M expertise left him cold.

What was it about Tempest that set a torch to his libido?

"I almost hate to ask why I'd need an alibi for last

Saturday night." She swiveled away from her laptop to face him.

"I wanted to be damn sure you weren't my murderer before things started heating up between us." He downsized the S and M woman and clicked on a—surprise—totally nude chick. There hadn't been many nude photos on the site, but nudity wasn't prohibited by the guidelines either.

"I rescue animals from trash cans, for crying out loud. Why would I ever kill someone?" She huffed out a sigh before turning toward his computer screen and the naked babe whose body was admirable enough, but it wasn't the body he wanted to see. "And on another note, nothing is going to heat up between us."

"Things are already heating up." He reached for the errant lock of hair at Tempest's temple and coiled his finger through the curl. Silky and sexy, the sable strand clung to his skin as if it wanted to linger with him.

Around him.

"You're just getting hot and bothered because you've been reading about every sex fetish under the sun and now you're staring at a disrobed female with perfect breasts." She eased back from him, taking her sweet curves and soft brown waves a few more inches away.

"She's not the one making me hot and bothered." He stared into Tempest's surprised brown eyes, wondering how she could possibly ignore such a blatant come-on. Did she find it that difficult to believe he would be interested? "Tell me, Tempest, do you date much?"

"Is this question of a professional nature?" She tugged on her necklace in what he began to realize was a nervous gesture. Fondling the small pearl at the end of the gold chain, she slid the charm to the right and then to the left, back and forth.

He imagined that mesmerizing touch skimming across his skin instead. Back and forth.

"Yes and no. We were talking about your alibi, but then it made me remember your alibi was a date." He rescued the pearl from her twitching fingers. "It made me wonder if you go out much or if you have a significant other in your life."

She went utterly still as he replaced the necklace just below her collarbone, being careful not to actually touch her. He had the distinct impression that under Tempest's somewhat shy facade lay a woman of emotions as fiery as her name implied. If he ever touched her…sparks would definitely fly.

"I don't have time for significant others." She shrugged, the movement shifting the pearl along her skin. "I barely have time to watch my soap opera and feed my dog."

"So the coffee shop guy doesn't hold any special place in your affections?" Not that he was jealous, damn it.

"I don't date." She said it more firmly, perhaps reading some of his intent in his eyes. "And I don't think you can find people who will be remotely compatible with you by hanging out in your average nightclub or coffee shop. I always thought a service like MatingGame would be the better way to go."

"You can't test chemistry online." He couldn't imagine meeting a woman in such a sterile environment. How would you know what the personal dynamics would be like unless you met face-to-face? Much better to get close.

"Chemistry is overrated. What about common interests and shared values? That's the heart of a great relationship."

Wes had heard the same spiel from his partner Vanessa, but had never given her ideas the time of day. Now that Tempest seemed to place stock in them, too, he wondered how a man would go about winning over her mind as much as her body.

Not that it should matter to Wes. His plans for Tempest were simple. Straightforward. Soon to be satisfying.

"Maybe you're right." He turned back to the computer, thinking he'd finish a little business at the same time he got to know Tempest better. "I thought I'd play around with the MatingGame application form anyway to get an idea what they want to know to match people up with dates. You want to help me? Maybe we can learn a few things about each other."

"We don't need to know much about each other to work together."

Undeterred, Wes started filling in blanks on the application form. "Qualities I value in a woman— loyalty, faithfulness, integrity."

Beside him, Tempest snorted.

"What?"

"What do you mean 'what'? You sound like you're shopping for a dog, not a girlfriend. Everybody wants loyalty in a relationship, Wes. That doesn't say squat about what kind of woman you'd like."

He stared at his application, still liking his answers. "This is the stuff that matters."

"What about creativity and vision? What about finding a woman who follows her dreams and celebrates life? Someone who isn't afraid to thumb her nose at conventional norms so she can immerse herself in her art…" She trailed off, her tawny gaze suddenly a bit horror-stricken.

Wes couldn't help the smile that curled his lips. He leaned in closer to Tempest, ready to find out if she harbored passion and fire beneath her nervous twitches and tendency to wriggle.

"Someone like you?"

5

TEMPEST COULDN'T ANSWER. Couldn't think. Couldn't make herself move away from the six-foot-plus detective inching closer to her with every breath.

If she had reasons for keeping her distance from this man, she certainly couldn't remember them now when her whole body shivered in anticipation of whatever might come next.

His lips brushed hers in a whisper-light caress, just enough to whet her appetite for more. She caught the scent of peppermint tea on his breath and spicy aftershave on his jaw, her senses focusing solely on Wes until the rest of the room around her disappeared. She could only taste this moment, this man.

Sliding her hands up his shoulders, she absorbed the feel of him the way she would test a new batch of clay. Except Wes was already perfectly formed and sharply defined, chiseled by more skilled fingers than her own. She eased her way up his corded neck, molding her hands about his strong jaw until she pulled him closer, deepening the kiss.

He was beautiful. Her hands recognized the

physical appeal of his cleanly defined muscles, savoring the supple skin over hard, rippled strength. But the delights for her hands couldn't come close to the feast for her mouth. His kiss teased and invited, daring her to give more of herself to him.

She hoped she knew better, because the languid strokes of his tongue tempted her to fall right into him. Breathe him in. Experience firsthand the most amazing sculpture imaginable.

She skimmed her fingers into his dark hair, winding them around his neck. He growled deep in his throat, encouraging her.

Until he kept on growling.

Arching back, she broke their kiss. Only to discover Eloise doing the growling a scant foot away, her ruff raised in aggressive warning as she snarled softly at Wes.

"No, Eloise," Tempest scolded her, using the stern voice the doggie-school instructor had taught her. "Go lay down."

Eloise cocked her head first to one side and then the other—clearly confused.

"She thinks I was devouring you," Wes supplied, keeping still until the dog trotted off to her open kennel where Tempest kept her blanket and a few toys.

"She's my voice of reason." Tempest knew she should listen to the dog instead of her sex-deprived libido, but Wes didn't make it easy. "And I would think she did you a favor."

"By making sure I didn't get past first base?" His softened tones brought to mind pillow talk and breakfast in bed. "How do you figure?"

She shut out the sound of that seductive voice in an effort to keep her distance. Maintain space. Remember that he suspected a business she'd brought on board at Boucher.

"Kissing me only complicates things for you. For all you know, I'm selling my fellow sisters on the street for a few quick bucks." Growing more indignant by the moment, she straightened in her chair, easing away from him. Where was his sense of honor, for crying out loud?

Wes rolled his eyes. "Whoever is behind this isn't selling anyone on the street. If my informant is right, anything connected to MatingGame would be very high-end."

"Earth to Wes—that's all the more reason you should suspect me. My whole lifestyle is very high-end." She looked around her unassuming little studio with a thirteen-inch TV and a futon couch she'd dressed up with extra pillows. "Okay, so maybe I don't look too sophisticated around here, but you know perfectly well I come from a ridiculously privileged family."

"Who's the cop here anyway? Will you trust me to do my job? I've got great instincts about who to suspect, and frankly, you seem a little too unfamiliar with threesomes to run a call-girl operation." He tipped back in his chair, drumming his hands on his chest. "Besides, when it comes right down to it, I'm not investigating MatingGame, *per se*. I'm only interested in how it relates to my murder case."

"So I should feel fine about you kissing me because you would never have to be the one to bust me?"

"You should feel fine about kissing me because I make you feel damn good."

Was she that transparent? She suppressed the urge to run her finger over her lips that still tingled from his kiss. "Do you always say what you think?"

"Hell no. I've been a detective for nine years, so there have been plenty of times I can't say what I think. Would I have a job that long if I pointed fingers at people and told them they were guilty as hell?" He tugged a curl at her shoulder and watched it spring back into place. "I've got to reserve my professional opinion, but I make snap judgments on a personal level just like everybody else. I know better than to share them."

"Really?" She noticed the ivy tattoo around his wrist and reminded herself to ask him about it. "Does that mean you have personal opinions about me you're not sharing, even though you have no problem telling me how *I* feel?"

His eyebrows shot up. "Lady, what you don't know about men is a lot."

"Didn't I say I don't date much?" Since her father had been too busy wheeling and dealing his way through life, Tempest had learned much of what she knew about men from soap operas. And while she adored her TV heroes, most of the men she met in real life didn't have secret identities, evil twins with ties to underworld gangs or sordid pasts in which they were raised by Gypsies.

"But you've heard the stat that men think about sex something like every ten minutes, right?"

"I thought it was every half hour."

He shrugged, his T-shirt shifting along with his sculpted muscles. "It's a lot. If you take that into account, you can probably guess that men spend an inordinate amount of time thinking about women. Yet I haven't shared any of those thoughts with you."

"Sex thoughts?" The air in the apartment suddenly seemed thick. Heavy. She breathed in the male scent of him and remembered the taste of his mouth.

"Definitely." He turned back to the computer abruptly. "In fact, as long as I'm thinking major sex thoughts, I might as well enter my profile into the computer to see what MatingGame comes up with as a match for me."

"You want to find a date?" Annoyed, she wondered how he could channel sexual energy so easily from one woman to another.

"I want to see if the system pairs me up with a legitimate date or a woman expecting to get paid for her favors." He tapped into the Blind Date section of the site. "But the only section of the company that could really orchestrate something like this would be the Blind Date service."

Intrigued, Tempest watched him fill out the form about what he looked for in a woman. Interestingly, he deleted his ideas about loyalty and faithfulness.

"You want a woman who takes pleasure in her femininity and isn't afraid to show it off." Tempest puzzled over the words, coming up with only a vague image in her mind. "You mean someone who wears short skirts?"

She really hoped he wasn't that tacky. Still, she couldn't staunch the urge to peer down at the long cotton dress she's tossed on this morning because it covered her from head to toe. The fashion equivalent of body armor.

"No. Although short skirts are never a bad thing." A dimple puckered into his cheek even though he didn't crack a smile. "I thought it would be too cheesy to say I'd like a woman with a closetful of lingerie."

Remembering the mounds of silk and lace strewn all over her apartment the day before, Tempest shrank deeper into her chair. "Very cheesy. Women want to be respected for their brains."

Although being drooled over for their bodies wasn't necessarily a bad thing, either. Especially if Wes Shaw happened to be the drooler in question.

Geez, what was she thinking? Thank God she hadn't worn a short skirt. She needed a cynical cop in her life like she needed a few more years in the corporate world. No, thank you.

"But now that I think about it, if I want to test the waters to see if there are women using this service to find paying customers, maybe I'd be better off sounding sex-starved. Cheesy may be the way to go." He continued typing away, finally turning the monitor toward her when he finished so she could see what he had written.

Tempest scanned the parts she'd already read, wondering what he'd thought of her heaps of lingerie scattered around her apartment yesterday. Had he been curious about the fact that there were ten times as many camisoles on the carpet as sweaters?

She happened to really enjoy lingerie.

"Must like dogs?" She couldn't help but focus on the one other characteristic she shared with Wes's cheesy dream woman.

"That's too honest, isn't it?" He tapped his finger along the delete key to get rid of his last line.

"And you honestly want a woman who likes dogs?"

"I've got Kong, remember? She's a St. Bernard, so she tends to scare off all but the most adamant of dog lovers."

There was something reassuring about a guy who had a pet. He could care for something. And chances were he had low blood pressure, right? Pet owners couldn't be too fussy or uptight. "A St. Bernard?"

"I know—you think it's too big for a city apartment, right?"

"Heck, no. I just say that because everybody automatically tells me I shouldn't keep Eloise cooped up in here with me and I'm tired of hearing it."

They compared dog notes, shared frustrations of hair on their favorite clothes and agreed a dog made the Sunday morning trek for the newspaper way more fun.

And somehow, Tempest really wished she'd be on the receiving end of his blind date.

"Are you really going to submit that form?" She wasn't sure if he'd been serious, or if he just wanted to see what kinds of questions the program generated.

"Of course. I need to talk to the woman in charge of MatingGame, but until then, it might help me fig-

ure out whether or not the business is legitimate."
And before she could say another word about it, he
clicked the send button to launch his dating criteria
into cyberspace.

Surprise made her stare at the computer even after
the form disappeared. "But you won't actually go on
the date?"

"Depends." He shut down the screen and
swiveled his chair toward her. "Right now I'm only
interested in one woman."

Tempest held her breath while she waited to find
out who that might be. Like a Friday afternoon cliff-
hanger, he left her tense. Anxious. And so much
more intrigued than she should be.

But no matter what he said, Tempest knew she
couldn't let him stay.

WES TRACED HIS THUMB down the her soft cheek,
knowing he couldn't let her push him aside like she
seemed to shove away everything else in her life. She
wasn't close to her family and didn't enjoy being
part of her father's business so she lived a secret life
in Chelsea when she wasn't a corporate executive.

He liked Tempest. She didn't put on airs. Didn't
pretend to be something she wasn't. And after
women he'd dated in the past, he found that kind of
honesty intriguing.

Hell—to be honest with *himself*—he hadn't
found anything about women intriguing during the
rough months since they found his first partner's
body. So the fact that Tempest Boucher made him
sit up and take notice was a major event.

He just didn't want to let her know it or he had the feeling she'd run far and fast.

"I think I've made it obvious I'd like to get to know you better." He'd let his kiss say as much, hadn't he? "But when it comes to my job, I can't afford to overlook any avenue that will achieve my ends. I need to know what's going on at MatingGame and Blind Date seems like the only place on the site that might allow a hooker to ply her trade."

"You think your killer could be working alone? Maybe this woman doesn't go through any kind of service." Tempest remained very still as he touched her cheek.

Wes couldn't afford to encourage the hope in her eyes. "I doubt it. Most women in the business know that's not a safe way to work."

"So you'll test the Blind Date service personally." She raised an eyebrow, clearly disapproving of his methods. Still, she didn't take him to task for it, instead turning her attention to his hand. "Neat tattoo."

He stared down at the green ivy snaking around his wrist. "It was a good save."

"A save?" She wrinkled her nose. "What do you mean?"

"I tattooed an old girlfriend's name on my wrist and came to regret it when she cheated on me with another guy. But I went back to the shop and the artist managed to transform 'Belinda' into a chain of ivy." He'd actually asked for poison ivy at the time, using a twenty-two-year-old's logic that tying yourself to a woman was the equivalent of a bad rash. Luckily, the tattoo lady had ignored him and produced something a little tamer.

Being a horticultural nimrod, Wes didn't even know he'd gotten English ivy instead of the poison variety until a year later.

"Can you imagine?" Tempest shook her head, her brown curls hopping around her shoulders. "How could anyone be so greedy to need two men at once? I never understood the rationale behind cheating. If you want out of a relationship, just tell the other person. Is that so hard?"

"Careful, lady, or I'll start thinking you're harboring a big store of loyalty and faithfulness and all those things you assured me I could only find in a canine."

"I mold penises for a living, remember?" Her teasing tone made it clear she didn't want any part of a serious conversation. "You can't trust a woman who hunts down naked men to model for her."

He knew damn well she was yanking his chain. What could it hurt to yank back?

"Really?" Rising, he reached for the hem of his T-shirt. "I've been looking for an excuse to get naked with you. Why don't you give me your professional opinion?"

He waited for her to say no. Stop. Keep your clothes on. Anything. But as his T-shirt hit the floor and his hands reached for the button on his jeans, he wondered if maybe Tempest Boucher hadn't been bluffing at all.

She watched him in fascinated silence—hell, he

hoped it was fascinated and not horrified—her eyes lingering on every inch of exposed skin. And suddenly, blood whooshed through him so fast he was halfway to having a heart attack and an erection that would be evident from two miles away.

Damnation. What kind of stupid-ass idiot started peeling off his clothes around a woman he hardly knew? A woman he really wanted?

Her avid gaze fell to the hard-on that could have been a circus attraction. Eyes going wide, she yanked her attention up to his face, cheeks flushed.

"I don't really hire naked models," she informed him, breathless. Coming to her feet, she tucked strand after strand of brown hair behind her ear.

"It's okay, I don't charge." He found himself stepping closer, incapable of exerting the effort required to keep his distance any longer. The circus erection had only gotten larger when those honey-brown eyes of hers caressed him.

Perhaps the size of his member should have alerted him to the fact that blood was no longer flowing to his brain. But then, his thinking was seriously impaired.

"Speaking strictly from a creative standpoint, I'm impressed." The single pearl she wore around her neck rose and fell with every rapid breath.

"What about from a personal standpoint?" He stopped an inch away from her, breathing in her scent, which he'd begun to recognize as almond.

He wouldn't step any closer without some sort of invitation. A sign.

"Personally speaking?" Now that her hair had

been firmly tucked behind her ear, she pulled a strand forward and twisted it around her finger. "I might need more information before I can form an opinion."

"Ask away." He didn't mean to lean forward, but he must have—or she must have—because the soft fabric of her long, cotton dress brushed his chest.

His eyes crossed at the contact, her lush breasts tempting him beyond reason.

Still, she held back. She bit her lip as she seemed to struggle with her thoughts, her face a picture of sensual distress.

When she finally opened her mouth to speak, she murmured a quiet, "What the hell?" before she moved closer. Her hands landed on his waist to skim around his back. "Maybe I just need to feel for myself."

Heat flashed through him like a thunderbolt. His arms banded around her, dragging her into him. Her mouth opened beneath his, soft and warm and so damn inviting. He cupped her head to find the perfect angle, fingers stroking through her thick curls until he found the vulnerable stretch of her neck.

She arched into him, generous curves pressing against him. He wanted his hands everywhere at once, hungry to know the feel of her. Her dress swirled around his calves, clinging to the fabric of his jeans. A blend of soft textures assailed his senses—her hair, her skin, that dress of hers all begged to be touched. Everything about Tempest drew him closer, invited him to linger.

"Wes."

The sound of his name reached his ears, the only discernible word amid breathy sighs and the gentle smack of their lips.

Easing back, he peered down at her in the halo of light emitted by the computer screen, her apartment grown dark in late afternoon thanks to the short winter day.

"Too fast?" He hadn't meant to spin the kiss out, make it so important. But his good intentions had fled when she stared at him with those dark, hungry eyes of hers, and then once he'd kissed her—his body seemed to remember exactly how long it had been since he'd kissed anyone like he meant it.

"No." Shaking her head, her curls bounced restlessly. "Yes. Maybe. I just—"

Prying himself further away, he skimmed his hands up to the safer terrain of her shoulders. "You tasted so good, and it's been a long time for me. Sorry if I rushed you."

"It's not that." Her fingers alighted on his chest briefly, then skittered away again. "I welcomed the kiss and the ah—view."

He resisted a juvenile urge to flex for her. "My pleasure."

"But I don't think you realize what you'd be getting yourself into if we…continue in that vein."

"On the contrary, I think I know exactly what I'd be getting myself into, and after the fireworks of one kiss, I can say with some assurance that anything more than that would rock my whole damn universe." No sense denying the obvious—he wanted her.

"I don't mean that." She reached to flick on a

desk lamp, bathing them in dim light. "I know that part would be great, but getting involved with me could be messy."

"I've already learned not to tattoo names on my wrist. What more do I need to know?"

"Every relationship I've ever had has been splashed all over the newspapers. Even taking in a movie with the coffee shop guy turned into a major ordeal, and you found out from him firsthand that it meant less than nothing." Huffing out a sigh, she blew a curl away from her eyes. "I just needed to warn you that hanging out with me will probably only lead to a big headache."

"We could keep things quiet." He traced the golden chain around her neck with his finger. "Private."

"Trust me, I've tried it. I couldn't even keep the results of my college final exams secret. My scores are still available on the Internet if you're interested, by the way."

Finally, Wes's brain began thinking again. Reason returned as he thought about his privacy vanishing the moment he started something with Tempest.

Could he afford to have his life served up for public consumption? Especially when he had a killer to catch?

"So you're willing to back away just because of the potential for a media splash?" Maybe she'd been thinking of him and trying to protect his private life. But what if she didn't want her well-known name linked with average Joe police detective?

He'd be willing to bet he wasn't the kind of man

the Boucher family had envisioned for their daughter, even for something short-term. They were megamillionaires with a bona fide fortune to oversee and connections around the globe.

And he was…trying to make the city safer, one crook at a time. Or at least he had been until he'd been forced to face facts that Steve was dead three months ago. He'd been in denial for a long time that his partner had really died, and once his body was found, Wes had been rethinking his job. But whether he decided to remain with the NYPD or move into something with a little less potential for shifting loyalties and career burnout, Wes knew he would never be the kind of man a socialite-turned-corporate-executive needed.

He wasn't sure if he was backing away now for himself or because he sensed she had her own agenda for putting up barriers between them. Either way, he needed to regroup before they made a move that could hurt them both.

"I think it's only fair to forewarn you of the consequences. Think what you want about me or Mating-Game, but I'd never purposely mislead anyone."

"Understood. And I appreciate the heads-up." He gathered a few papers he'd printed from the computer, hoping if he got some distance from her, he could make a decision without her almond scent fogging his brain.

Besides, he'd been serious about loyalty and honesty. They were a hell of a lot more important to him than creativity or access to millions of dollars. "I'll keep it in mind next time I get the urge to rip off my clothes around you."

Retrieving his shirt and the coat that he'd tossed over the chair, Wes jammed his arms through the holes and backed toward the door. They were from different worlds, damn it. Walking away from her shouldn't be so tough.

After exchanging quick goodbyes, he was out of her apartment and back on the street.

6

COULD THE MAN have sprinted off any faster?

Tempest decided even a hopeless optimist would have to agree that Wes couldn't wait to make tracks out of her apartment. He'd vanished as soon as she mentioned the possibility of media involvement, a surefire libido killer to most men.

Had she chased him away on purpose? Or had he been grateful for the excuse to reclaim a few more boundaries? She didn't know anymore, couldn't tell what had happened with her heart thumping like a pottery wheel overloaded with an uneven lump of clay. Why hadn't she paid better attention to what happened between them?

Whistling to Eloise, she gave the dog free run of the apartment again as she mindlessly clicked through some of the screens on the MatingGame site. If today had been a scene on her soap opera, she would have been damn certain Wes would return the following week to confuse her with more moral-melting kisses.

But this was real life, and she wasn't so sure he'd be back at all.

As regret stole over her, she found herself staring

at a new, blank application form for MatingGame's Blind Date service. Who had opened that file? Tapping her finger idly on the mouse, she stared at the questions and found herself mentally penning her answers.

What are your turn-ons? Ignoring the *Playboy* centerfold feel of the short interview section, Tempest started typing the first response that popped into her head. "Men who don't care what I do for a living. Men who are comfortable in their own skin. Men who know what they want and aren't afraid to go after it."

In your face, Wes Shaw.

If he couldn't be the kind of man she needed— and really, what business did she have dating the cop investigating MatingGame?—maybe she should go out and find someone else. Spending time in Wes's arms had made her realize how long it had been since she'd indulged in slow, deep, hot kisses.

So what if she couldn't imagine anyone else's kisses tasting so good, or firing her up half as much as the ones she'd experienced this afternoon? Maybe just this once she'd take her dating fate into her own hands by meeting someone outside her small circle of friends and business associates. Someone completely different from the handful of guys she'd dated in the past.

Through Blind Date, she could remain anonymous, which suited her needs perfectly. Now, any guy who chose her profile wouldn't be dating her for her family connections. Too often in her sparse dating history, men had only been interested in her for one thing and—disappointingly enough—it wasn't even sex.

This way she could find out for herself if the Internet dating business worked legitimately. In her gut, she knew it did, damn it. Still, wouldn't it be nice to have proof firsthand to wave in front of Wes Shaw's handsome face?

Filling out the rest of the form, Tempest submitted her application for her first ever Blind Date before she gave herself time to change her mind. Didn't the old saying preach that what was good for the goose was good for the gander?

With a little luck, maybe she'd find someone else to quench the slow burn Wes had started deep inside her.

DAYDREAMING HER WAY through a board meeting Monday morning, however, Tempest had to admit some things were easier said than done.

Put Wes out of her mind? She must have been engaged in some serious wishful thinking over the weekend if she thought she'd forget about the hottest kisses on the planet. After a day and a half of catching herself remembering Wes's touch, she had to admit that no stray guy she found through a dating service would match up to the red-hot detective investigating her intruder. Entering her profile in the Blind Date system had been a rash act she had no intention of actually following through on.

At this moment, fantasizing about Wes held far more appeal than listening to her board bicker about who to appoint as the next CEO of Boucher Enterprises, so she allowed her imagination to run free. She'd learned that being a good manager involved a fair amount of listening to other people's concerns. Or at least, allowing other people to vent their frustrations even if she wasn't listening quite as closely as she should.

Hands smoothing over the napkin beside her cooling cup of darjeeling, Tempest's gaze dropped to the expanse of shiny mahogany conference table while Kelly Kline, VP of global development, found one excuse after another for why Boucher should look internally for a CEO.

The general consensus among the board was that Kelly wanted the top slot for herself—a feat that wouldn't happen as long as Tempest had any input. Kelly thrived at her job as a public relations guru who spoke three languages and made frequent trips abroad. But she seemed a little too calculating for Tempest's tastes. Kelly had proven to be a corporate shark and a bit of a tyrant in her department, yet extremely effective.

Allowing the woman to have her say, Tempest's thoughts ran to having Wes Shaw at her mercy on the mahogany conference table. She could envision the dark, strong wood as a perfect backdrop for the detective's lean, sculpted muscles.

The private conference room was her stronghold, the one place in the world where she reigned supreme. Because even if Tempest didn't enjoy her stressful job all the time, at least her personal meeting space was familiar terrain and she could be in control here. The sensation was a welcome one after she'd felt so helpless during the weekend with her apartment trashed and her sculptures destroyed. Wes had practically taken over the place with his big, I'm-in-charge presence and his knowledge of catching criminals.

If he set foot in this facet of her world, he would see a very different woman. And next time, Tempest wouldn't give him the upper hand over her again. She might lick every delicious inch of that primo male form of his, but she'd be damn sure to remain in control of the situation.

Remembering his horror at holding the broken clay penis in his hand, Tempest wondered how her artwork measured up to the man. Was he as impressive as her fanciful imaginings? Judging by the eyeful she'd gotten Saturday evening, she'd have to answer with a resounding yes. And if she ever had the man at her disposal on the conference table, she would damn well find out for sure. If he started getting naked with her again, she would make certain he finished the job.

"Tempest?"

Kelly's voice intruded in her fantasies, an unwanted female in the middle of a very hot daydream.

Frowning, Tempest blinked. Remembered she was supposed to be listening sympathetically to Kelly's reasons for why the board shouldn't interview the latest CEO candidate someone had suggested.

"I think we need to come up with a solution before the month is out," Tempest offered, deciding the time had come to put her foot down. The longer she allowed the board to waffle, the longer the company stayed in limbo. And seeing all her artwork destroyed this weekend had made her realize where her real priorities lie. She should be working on her statues and honing her craft instead of operating in survival mode at Boucher. "I'd like to take a private ballot one month from today for who we should interview and I'll pull three candidates from the pool. We're long overdue settling this."

Amid a flurry of protests, Tempest ended the meeting, feeling more sure of herself than she had in a long time. She should have set a deadline and stuck to it months ago. Perhaps her weekend intruder had done her a little bit of a favor in spite of the threat and the rampant wreckage. At least the incident had strengthened her resolve to get her life in order.

The board members filed out while she dumped her cup of tea in the sink at a wet bar. For a minute she thought she'd given herself a shock when a sizzle of electricity shot through her with a definite jolt.

"Knock, knock." The unanticipated masculine voice behind her made her realize that the shock had been of the sexual variety.

Turning, she found Wes framed in the doorway between her office and private conference room. A dark khaki trench coat hugged his shoulders, the stiff fabric dotted with raindrops. The overcoat appealed to her daydreaming mind, making her realize how much she'd like to play cloak and dagger with this man.

Not just any man, curse his hide.

Only Wes.

How had she ever thought she could work up the nerve to accept a blind date with anyone else when Wes seemed to be the only man appealing to her unexpectedly ravenous libido?

"Isn't my assistant out front?" She fumbled with her teacup, spilling a few last drops on her thumb.

"That's a hell of a welcome." He stepped inside the room, taking the long way around the oversize conference table to peer around the meeting space. He took in the long windows looking out over the city, the skyscraper climbing higher than any of the buildings around it so that her window didn't look into another office, the way that so much Manhattan real estate did.

He ran his hand along the conference table as he approached, whistling appreciatively under his breath. "Nice place you have here."

His hand on the mahogany surface called forth images from her bold fantasies. The daydreams taunted her now, sending a rush of desire through her. Funny how she could picture being brash and brazen with Wes so much more easily when he wasn't actually in the room with her.

Coward.

Her conscience railing at her, she washed the tea off her hands and steadied herself. He was just a man, after all.

Just a sexy, appealing man who could kiss her into a near-orgasmic state.

"Thanks." She tugged at the silk scarf around her

neck, feeling a bit warm. "I'm just surprised to see you here since Rebecca usually fields all my appointments for me."

"I arrived bearing doughnuts and coffee. Maybe she forgot." He flashed her a disarming smile that would surely fluster the most dedicated of assistants.

Or maybe Rebecca simply thought she'd be doing Tempest a favor by providing her with a mouthwatering diversion to chase away the Monday morning doldrums.

"Can I get you anything?" Tempest opened the door of the minirefrigerator under the wet bar to reveal a wealth of soft drinks and flavored spring water. She might as well be civil, even if he had made it clear the other night that he wouldn't get involved with someone commanding such a prominent public profile. "I've got tea, if you like."

"No, thanks. That's not what I'm here for." Shrugging out of his coat, he folded the garment over one chair and then made himself comfortable in a large swivel seat at the head of the conference table.

Her seat.

"No?" She curbed her annoyance along with her lust, determined not to let either one show. Dropping into a chair midway down the table, she peered into her office and noticed the outer door had been shut, sealing them in complete privacy.

Had that been Rebecca's way of offering Tempest a few moments alone with Wes? Or had the gesture been Wes's attempt to sneak another kiss when he had no intention of giving her anything more substantial?

Neither answer soothed the increased tempo of her heart. She settled for simply casting him a level look and giving him her most businesslike board-room face. "Then how about you tell me what brings you here."

AN OVERWHELMING DESIRE to get you naked?

Somehow Wes didn't think she'd appreciate the answer after the way he'd lit out of her apartment Saturday night. Thankfully, he had another reason for showing up in her penthouse office this morning.

"I wanted to make sure you were having additional security installed in the Chelsea apartment. Whoever broke into your apartment used some finesse to pick your lock in a way that didn't damage the door at all. You need something more sophisticated to keep out today's crooks." It was a legitimate reason to see her again, right? He'd mentioned security to her over the weekend, but she'd been jittery on Friday and he hadn't trusted that she fully comprehended the importance of the message.

Then by Saturday he'd had more on his mind than safety, a professional error he wouldn't be making again. He'd even taken the liberty of locking her office door behind him on the way in. Not that he really anticipated anyone coming after her on the most elite floor of corporate offices in the building, but it couldn't hurt to be safe.

Private.

Ah, hell, who was he kidding? He'd bolted the door in case she had the urge to take up where they'd left off on Saturday. He might not like the idea of her high-profile career and status as a social figure putting him in the public eye, but he didn't stand a chance at getting her out of his head. By Sunday night he'd realized he just needed to find more creative solutions to their problem of too much publicity because he wanted her too much to concern himself with the inconvenience of his mug in the paper on occasion.

Locking doors behind them seemed like a good place to start today.

"I called a security company this morning. They're going to come by tomorrow to install something." She shifted in her seat just enough to make the leather chair squeak.

And remind Wes of the restless way she'd brushed up against him when they sat at her computer together over the weekend. His body revved at the memory of her scent. Her nearness. He couldn't deny he wanted that again along with a whole lot more.

"They couldn't come out today?" He'd driven by her building twice last night, uneasy with the idea of her alone in apartment 35, guarded only by Eloise. And if he'd entertained a few fantasies involving Ms. Boucher while he was at it, that was his business.

"They already juggled around their schedule just to get out tomorrow." Sitting straighter, she folded her hands together as if to keep herself still. "Is there anything else I can help you with, Detective? I have a busy schedule today."

Her tone verged on frosty, but not nearly chilly

enough to cool him off. Memories of their shared kiss had him in a state of perpetual simmer ever since he'd walked out of her apartment.

She looked different today in her executive suite than she had in her Chelsea apartment. She wore a vivid blue suit with a yellow silk scarf tucked into the neckline of her buttoned jacket. Tailored and sophisticated, the suit screamed high-powered exec, but Wes's eyes kept straying to the scarf as he speculated about what she wore beneath the jacket.

A blouse? Some kind of lingerie top like he'd seen strewn all over her apartment? Or nothing at all?

Aside from the sexy mystery of the jacket, her clothes now weren't all that unlike the ones she'd been wearing when they first met. Maybe it was the setting today, or just her attitude that seemed more cool and in-control. But there was a definite difference in her.

"I wanted to see if anything had turned up missing at your place now that you've had more time to look around."

"Nothing." She crossed her ankles beneath her chair, her weekend running shoes replaced by camel-colored leather pumps. "I don't think anything was stolen. All the intruder's effort seems to have been geared toward destruction."

Wes didn't like that one damn bit. "All signs point to the break-in being a threat, probably perpetrated by someone who has a particular beef with you. We didn't find any prints but yours around the apartment, so whoever trashed the place took time to cover their tracks."

Perhaps he'd finally succeeded in scaring her because she nodded with jerky movements, her fingers smoothing the scarf at her neck.

"I won't work at the studio anymore until the security is installed. I usually sleep at the family house during the week anyway."

"Good." He hated upsetting her, but there could be no help for it. "And hopefully we'll have some answers soon on MatingGame. I'm trying to set up a time to meet a date tomorrow night and we'll see if the service works as advertised."

"You're going on the date?" Color returned to her cheeks, her twitchy fingers stilling over her scarf.

"Since your Web mistress never got in touch with me, it's the fastest way to get the answers we need."

"Apparently Bliss Holloway's mother has been in poor health and Bliss is out of touch. I'm sure we'll hear from her soon." Tempest sounded aggravated and looked downright mad.

She couldn't be upset about the date? Maybe she was just annoyed he continued to check into her company, because his brain refused to consider that she could be…jealous?

The idea fanned the slow heat that had been building inside him all weekend long.

"Until then, I guess I'm going on a blind date." He looked back through her office toward her locked door. They were utterly alone, the conference room inaccessible to anyone else. Wicked thoughts came to mind. "Too bad *we* couldn't have enjoyed that kind of anonymity."

She stared back at him blankly for a moment

until her honey-colored eyes narrowed. "What do you mean?"

"I mean, wouldn't it have been fun if we could have met under different circumstances?" He eased out of his seat at the head of the table and closed the distance between them, propelled toward her by a deep hunger he didn't fully understand. Halting a few inches away from her, he dropped into a swivel chair right next to her. "What would it have been like between us if I wasn't the cop investigating your company and you weren't a woman I needed to protect?"

Her fingers splayed on the mahogany conference table, her red nails as shiny as the richly polished wood. She stared down at her hand on the table for a long moment before meeting his eyes.

"It might have been very interesting," she admitted, voice soft with sensual promise.

Or was that hopeful thinking on his part?

The air around them turned warm and heavy. The raindrops that had soaked his hair and his coat seemed to evaporate in a slow hiss of steam as their bodies inched closer.

He reached for the length of yellow and blue silk around her neck, gently tugging the scarf from her jacket in one smooth, deliberate motion. She sat perfectly still as he watched the fabric uncoil from her skin.

No blouse beneath.

Just incredible cleavage and creamy smooth skin. Savoring the warm scent of the scarf that had shielded her breasts, Wes rubbed the fabric between his fingers and allowed a darkly erotic idea to take shape in his mind.

A way to accommodate their wish for anonymity.

"Maybe we can still have our own blind date," he whispered the suggestion that had been hovering around his brain, urging him to find a way to be with her. Skimming the silk up her cheek, he twined the material around her eyes. "A few stolen moments with no identities attached if your schedule allows."

When she didn't move so much as a muscle, he allowed himself to secure the cloth behind her head, tying it in a lazy knot.

While he waited for the full import of his suggestion to sink in, he studied the way she looked with the impromptu blindfold wrapped around her eyes. Wild brown curls escaped from beneath the fabric, the bright color of the scarf highlighting the pale perfection of her cheek. But as he watched, a tinge of hectic color brightened the exposed portion of her face. A rosy blush? Or the sensual flush of a woman slowly becoming turned on?

Her lips worked silently for a moment, as if she couldn't quite come to terms with what she wanted to say. The gesture drew his gaze, and sent a rush of heat southward. He thought about what it would be like to personally lick off every last bit of her lipstick before he explored her mouth, the unique taste of her, for hours on end.

"I've got appointments today," she finally managed, although the sighed sentiment didn't sound much like a protest. She wound her finger in one loose end of the scarf that draped carelessly over her shoulder.

"I warned your assistant my business with you might take precedence over everything else." Laying his finger along her lower lip, he stroked the soft fullness of her mouth. "And I locked the door."

The nutty almond fragrance she wore seemed all the more intense as the heat between them cranked up. Tempest nipped his finger before drawing it into her mouth and swirling her tongue around the digit.

His eyes were already crossing when she finally nodded. "Maybe you're on to something with this anonymous thing. But *you're* not wearing a blindfold."

Lowering his damp finger to the valley between her breasts, Wes traced a wet line over her ample curves.

"That's okay. I'm getting off on watching you wear one." The trace of moisture on her full lips was killing him. "And by now I've already forgotten everything we were talking about except how much I want you."

A hum of pleasure escaped her lips before she came up out of her chair and landed in his lap, her knees straddling his thighs.

The heat that had been on slow burn inside him all weekend roared into a full-fledged blaze as her compact curves and creamy legs arrived within reach. Her acquiescence was an unexpected gift. A tempting treasure.

An unbelievable freaking moment he wouldn't ever forget.

And he planned to savor every square inch of her, starting right now.

7

THERE WAS no stopping her now.

Tempest's bravado seemed to have increased ten-fold the moment Wes wrapped the silk scarf around her eyes, relegating her world to a place of touches and tastes. The scent of his rain-dampened skin, the feel of his hands skating over her hips, drove her to the point of no return.

She'd been daydreaming about this an hour ago, and now that he was here, in the flesh, she planned to fulfill her fantasies just this once. Her appointments could damn well wait until another day.

Palms sliding beneath her jacket, Wes smoothed his thumb over her bare waist. She'd always been self-conscious of her curves, even more so after a candid photo of her dancing at a friend's wedding ran in the social pages with a caption implying she must have really enjoyed the bride's cake. But her admittedly ample curves didn't seem like such a bad thing when Wes got hold of them. His fingers sank into her softness, urging her closer to his lap and all the enticing male heat waiting for her there.

"You're sure you're okay with this?" Wes's voice wove through her steamy thoughts, his lips brushing her ear as he spoke. "I don't want to cause a professional flap for you."

She wouldn't allow him to stop. Not now when her mind swam with sensual imaginings, her body more in tune to his touch than it had ever been for any other man's.

"I dedicated twenty hours a day to this company for months on end after my father died." She didn't regret the time since it had given her a chance to finally understand the man who had always been too busy for her when he was alive. She'd come to peace with Ray Boucher in that time. But she wouldn't bury her own needs for the sake of the company forever. "I'm entitled to a few hours of downtime."

If she hadn't been blindfolded, her increased senses might not have picked up the low rumble of approval that went clear through Wes. His body practically hummed with anticipation now, and she couldn't quite believe she possessed so much power over the man.

Consumed with the need to fulfill her daydream visions, she edged backward on the chair, ready to drag him with her toward the conference table. But then his hands found her thighs, his thumbs sliding upward on the inside of her legs until she remembered exactly how much of a barrier stood between her and Wes now that she'd straddled him. Only a tiny triangle of peacock-blue satin shielded her from his wandering touch.

Maybe she could wait to tackle him onto the conference table. Right now, she could only think about what he might do when he discovered the decadent lingerie beneath her conservative suit. Heat licked tiny tongues of flame up her thighs as he nudged the nubby cotton tweed hemline higher and higher.

Cool air breezed between her legs before his fingers touched her. She held herself still, sensing his gaze on her now exposed hips.

"You're gorgeous." His whispered reverence soothed any wounds left by unflattering photos or the occasional broken zipper on her skirts. She delved beneath his suit jacket to touch him through his crisp blue shirt. Fiery warmth radiated from his shoulders, a wealth of heat she couldn't absorb fast enough.

"You just caught me on a good day." She knew she was a far cry from celebrity-perfect, but he made her feel beautiful.

"I've been dying since Friday trying to picture you wearing this kind of stuff." Wes's finger traced the outline of one satin strap holding her delicate G-string in place.

Part of her wanted to whip off the blindfold to see his eyes on her, but somehow it seemed easier to be bold and adventurous this way. With the scarf to keep her in the dark, she could be as brash as any daytime TV diva determined to have her own way.

Licking a kiss along his jaw, Tempest whispered in his ear. "You know I've got lots more where this came from." She gave her hips a little shake to make sure he knew what she was talking about. "If you please me today, maybe you'll be seeing more in the future."

Hooking his finger into the satin strap, Wes tugged gently but didn't pull the panties off. "I'd like that."

"I'd like more of you, Detective." She tugged at his tie, savoring the slide of hot silk between her fingers as she undid the knot. "You seem to be getting all the visuals here."

Nimble, quick fingers went to work on her skirt buttons. "You can't get a visual when you're blindfolded anyway. Why not let me worry about what to see?"

"Only if you let me worry about what to touch." She dropped her hand to his fly, amazed at her audacity. She'd never been this way with a man.

Her palm fluttering over the ridge in his trousers made his fingers move faster on her skirt. And then she lost track of his touch at her waist as all her attention narrowed to the hard heat of him.

She shoved his coat off his shoulders and felt him shrug out of his suit jacket. Clothes peeled off them in every direction, her skirt slipping to her feet, her jacket falling open to expose the peacock-blue satin bra with sheer lace insets.

He sucked in a breath and she almost envied him the ability to see. But she wasn't ready to leave the safety of her blindfold yet, not when it infused her with so much delicious daring. The heat steaming off her skin warmed her perfume and supercharged the light, almond fragrance she wore.

"Like what you see?" She tugged on his belt, while he remained still

"Incredible." His voice hit a hoarse note as she

carefully unbuttoned his pants around an erection that would have made any woman's mouth water.

Although it wasn't her mouth going damp right now.

"I've been thinking about you today," she confided, easing his zipper down until his cock sprang free. "Even though I didn't want to."

He rolled the straps of her bra down her shoulders with his palms before lowering his lips to the curve of her neck. "I think I'm insulted."

"Don't be. In these fantasies of mine, you were very good." She shuddered as his lips roamed over the tops of her breasts, the low rumble of normal office conversation on the other side of one wall reminding her what a risk they took, although she knew no one would disturb her while her door remained closed. And no one would be able to hear her and Wes except maybe her office assistant.

But still…the others would know she'd been closeted with this sexy cop for hours and they would probably wonder.

"Then it wasn't a fantasy." He flicked off her bra and captured a nipple in his mouth. The hot sensation of his tongue swirling over her nearly brought her to her knees. "That must have been a premonition."

He shifted against her and there was a rustling sound before he picked her up and deposited her to sit on the conference table.

Squealing in surprise, she soaked in the feel of the cool mahogany surface beneath her, providing a stark contrast to the hot, lean muscles bending over her. His cock brushed her thigh and she could tell he must have discarded his trousers along the way. He stood in front of her, poised between her thighs.

She wanted him, wanted this, so badly. Part of her longed to tell him she'd like to see him stretched out on the conference table beneath her, but even with the blindfold she couldn't find the words.

Knowing she'd spent long enough in the dark anyhow, Tempest reached for the silk scarf around her eyes and nudged it up and off.

She blinked, her eyes adjusting to the bright fluorescent lighting overhead.

And oh. *Ooh.*

Wes naked was a sight to see. The carved muscle and flat abs appealed to her sculptor's eye, but the weapon he was carrying…yipes. His shaft was pointed her way and looked very ready to strike.

Scooting toward the edge of the table she made her way closer, her greedy flesh hungry for a taste of him. He reached for her panties and snapped the skinny elastic straps, rendering her naked with a flick of his wrist. She leaned back on her arms to support herself, desperate to feel him inside her.

Her finger brushed a paper—no, a foil condom package he must have left on the table. Falling on it gratefully, she ripped it open with her teeth while she silently applauded his foresight. She was so far gone now, she wasn't entirely sure she would have remembered to be careful.

Rolling on the condom, she savored the length and size of him. He gripped her thighs, lifting her off the table until she slid her arms around his neck to hold on. He guided her closer, finding the perfect angle, and gently thrust his way inside.

Stretching around him, her body worked to accommodate his. He eased her back down to the table, settling her there so he could free his hands to touch her.

Eyes falling closed as he spread her with his fingers, Tempest shuddered from the wave of pleasure, a tiny foreshadow of the completion she knew would follow. The skill of his touch amazed her, his finger zeroing in on her clit again and again, even as he moved inside her with long, devastating strokes. She opened her eyes to see his burning into her with enough heat to singe her very soul.

Confusion and pleasure tangled inside her, startling her with how much she wanted this man. He was giving her everything he had, his deft touch taking her swiftly to the highest of sensual peaks, and yet she wanted even more...

Sealing her mouth to his, she kissed away her doubts, her fears, until only the heat remained. Her fingers sank into his skin, clinging, as he played between her thighs. His hips ground against hers, filling her so completely she thought she'd fly right apart.

Waves of pleasure crashed over her, pummeling her with their intensity. Her thighs locked, squeezing him tight to her until his release claimed him, too. Their shouts mingled, breathless and raw, bodies seizing with aftershocks. Lights danced behind her eyes, a star-studded spectacular just for her. She'd never had an orgasm like that. Not even close.

She almost hated to open her eyes and end this moment in case she never felt that way again. A depressing thought.

Wes's arms coming around her waist saved her from having to make that decision, however. He readjusted her, lifting her off the table where she'd somehow fallen back in a slump, his hands cradling her from the hard mahogany surface.

"Are you okay?" His voice, filled with more tender concern than she'd expected from a man of hard edges, warmed her insides.

She knew that kind of thinking was downright dangerous. As a closet romantic nursing a hunger for soap operas, Tempest knew that real life didn't operate the way she wanted. Therefore, sexy, honorable men like Wes Shaw could never be expected to fork over a bouquet of daisies and start a courtship just because they had wild sex on her conference room table.

Far from it.

The man who had run at the first hint of too much publicity was probably already busy looking for the door. Forcing herself to keep things light between them, she drew in a stabilizing breath.

"Just a little dazed, I think." Smiling with as much composure as she could manage, Tempest pried her eyes open. "That was something else, Detective."

HELL YEAH it was something else. Something out of this world and off his personal record books. Something completely unexpected and mind-blowing. It also happened to be eye-crossing, bone-incinerating and brain-scrambling.

Not that he planned to share any of that with Tempest.

"Damn straight it was." He kissed her, more than happy to allow the heat between them to do his talking for him. "You think anybody heard us?"

"Only Rebecca. And I didn't hire her because she can type fast." She eased up, her naked body brushing his and making him want her all over again. "She's my assistant because we went to school together. I've never had a tryst in my office before, but I trust her to keep all my secrets."

Prying himself away from her before he pushed her back against the table all over again, Wes scouted around for clothes. Did it make him an awful person that he was grateful for the office setting that prohibited intimate post-coital conversations? Not that he wouldn't have appreciated the chance to hold Tempest's body against his a little longer. But the level of their sex connection had thrown him for a major loop.

"Good." He tossed her a skirt while he zipped up. "I meant what I said before about not wanting to cause a stir for you. I didn't expect things to get so…out of hand here."

"Yet you arrived bearing prophylactics." She shrugged into her jacket before retrieving her scarf. "You were well-prepared for a man who didn't expect to get carried away."

Busted.

"Okay. Correction—I *wanted* something to happen, but I didn't think it would happen in the middle of your conference room." He watched her wind the scarf around her neck, carefully tucking the ends into her jacket to cover those incredible breasts of hers. Desire slugged through him as hot as if he hadn't just held her naked in his arms. "Nice view, by the way."

She glanced up, brown eyes wide.

Jerking a thumb toward the wall of windows high above any other building nearby, he dragged his gaze away from her centerfold curves to the panorama of downtown. "You've got great offices here. I can't imagine many buildings in the city rivaling this kind of view."

"You're full of it." She fluffed her dark curls around her face and then pushed a few strands behind one ear. "But thank you."

Her tone seemed different. Remote. Wes watched her, searching for a clue to her mood. She shuffled through some papers on her desk before slamming her appointment book closed.

"I guess I'm done here for the day if you want to walk down with me. I'll have to make up my missed appointments another day."

That was it? They'd just had the best sex of his life and now she wanted to dismiss him like one of her employees? He knew he had no right to be insulted since he'd been wondering how to avoid awkward after-sex conversations himself, but damn, even he wouldn't have tried rolling out the door that fast.

Still, he didn't have any intention of letting her out of his sight just yet.

"I'll walk you down. Better yet, I'll give you a lift back to your family's home." He would make sure she didn't try to stay at her apartment tonight, not until the security system was up and running. "You said Park Avenue, right?"

"Wait a minute." Tempest held out a restraining hand, blocking his exit with a manicured hand to his chest.

"What?"

"I thought you didn't want any part of the public eye." She slid her hand down and away. It surprised Wes how much he mourned the loss of that fleeting touch.

"I'm a cop escorting you home. That's the NYPD doing a damn fine job, and believe me, the good stuff never makes its way into the papers." When rumors had flown about the possibility of his former partner turning bad while undercover, however, the media couldn't shovel up dirt fast enough.

"You know as well as I do that no journalist in the world is going to take that angle." She shut down a coffee machine and flicked off the harsh fluorescent lights. It was only late afternoon, but already the late winter sky outside was hazy and gray. "As soon as they find out who you are and that we come from different walks of social life, they'll either paint a picture of me as a gullible heiress getting taken by a studly fortune hunter, or they'll intimate that I must be slumming it for a little while. I guarantee neither version is going to flatter to us."

No kidding. He could feel his nose already out of joint, his shoulders tense. "And you don't like being viewed as gullible or slumming, I take it?"

"Frankly, I don't care. I'm used to it, and I've

learned not to buy any newspaper besides the *Wall Street Journal* so I don't have to see things that upset me." She moved from the conference room into her office and straightened a few papers while shutting down her computer. "But I don't want to subject anyone else to that kind of scrutiny without ample warning."

"Consider me warned." He appreciated the heads-up, but even knowing the downside of dating her, he couldn't seem to talk himself out of it. He wanted her anyway.

On the plus side of things—Tempest didn't seem to care about media flack for her own sake. She wasn't embarrassed to be seen on the arm of your everyday, average cop. Some of the tension in his neck eased. "And if you think I'm studly after a quickie on the conference table, just wait until you see what I can do when I have more time."

"What makes you think you'll ever have another chance, Detective?" She arched a delicate eyebrow and failed to hide a smile.

"I'm on to you now." He tugged at her scarf as she pushed the button for a private elevator that stopped in her office. "You might look like an uptown girl, but you've got downtown, kinky tastes all the way. You can bet I'll find more ways to use that against you."

Her breath hitched just enough to make him want to kiss her again, but the elevator chose that moment to announce its arrival with a short chime. They left the building via her high-speed express car that took them directly to street level.

Her world probably boasted plenty of professional perks he couldn't even wrap his head around, another little reminder of how different they were.

As if her warning about the media hadn't damn well been bad enough. He'd barely had time to wonder how they would face that kind of attention when the elevator doors opened in the lobby and cameras flashed in his face. A crush of reporters moved toward them, although Wes could only make them out in silhouette thanks to the blind spots dancing around his vision. Questions fired at them from all sides while portable floodlights drowned them in a white-hot blaze.

"Do you know who broke into your apartment, Tempest?" A woman's shrill voice shouted from the crowd.

"Who's your friend, Tempest?" Another voice—gruff and male—assailed Wes's ears.

"Is it true police are investigating one of Boucher's companies?"

Still partially blinded, Wes barreled his way into the throng, figuring anyone dumb enough to plant themselves in front of an elevator deserved the trampling. How could she live with this kind of personal invasion all the time?

"No comment." He barked out the same words ten times over as he called on old college football skills to block and dodge his way through the crowd of camera-happy reporters and so-called journalists. Amazing what constituted news these days.

Tucking Tempest under his arm, he protected her the same way he'd protected the ball on numerous carries down the backfield in the days when life hadn't been so complicated. Although he was guessing she wouldn't appreciate the pigskin comparison, the tactic worked beautifully. She was in the end zone—his car, rather—in no time.

He slid into the driver's seat in time to see her pulling down the visors and turning her head to the side, obviously a pro at deflecting media attention. Shoving his unmarked Ford into gear, he drove uptown.

"Short of beating them off with a stick, I'd say we handled that as best as could be expected, wouldn't you?" He relaxed into his seat as they put a few blocks between themselves and Tempest's inquisitors.

"You sound like you enjoyed it." Only then did he detect the subtle sniffle behind her words.

"Are you upset?" He flipped the visors back up to get more light in the car so he could see her better in the twilight of a short winter's day. She looked a little glassy-eyed. Hell, yeah, she was upset. He'd been too busy playing his position to notice. "I just assumed you didn't want to talk to them about the case, so I figured you'd want to get out of there posthaste."

"Of course I did. I'm just sorry you had to deal with it." She cast a dire look across the front seat. "They've obviously discovered my connection to the studio in Chelsea now. You realize they'll know who you are by tomorrow morning's early edition, right?"

"I don't care." At least, not as much as he'd expected he would. Besides, he'd seen firsthand that she could use his help dodging reporters, and somehow that put him more at ease.

"You don't?"

"I've been giving it some consideration, and I realized it doesn't really matter to me since it's not like I go undercover anymore. Having my name linked to one of the most gorgeous women in the city isn't exactly going to hurt my reputation." Although the guys at the precinct would have a field day with Wes's face in the social pages. No doubt there would be a hundred copies of it pasted around his desk by morning—with appropriate comic book detailing and thought-bubble commentary, of course. "You just caught me off guard the other night when you brought up the media spotlight. Sort of blew my mind, I guess. Now, where on Park Avenue?"

She gave him an address that put her overlooking Central Park—a ritzy privilege possessed by very few. Maybe some of his thoughts showed on his face because she hurried to explain.

"It's a little ostentatious, but it was my parents' choice, not mine. My folks stayed there until Mom decided she needed a whole new continent to escape my dad and bought a flat in London. I lived away at school most of the time anyway, and then when my dad died, it was just me knocking around the whole huge place until I found the studio downtown." She stopped abruptly. "Sorry I'm rambling. The house has always intimidated me and no matter how long I wear the family name I think the Boucher brand of extravagance will always embarrass me."

Wes pulled up to the curb in front of a brick facade that screamed "Old New York" and stopped. The understated, elegant building didn't look ostentatious to him, but considering property values in this part of town, Wes knew it had to cost a small fortune. Especially since the family probably owned all ten floors. He knew downtown apartment buildings complete with doormen that were smaller than the Boucher place.

"What matters is that you're safe and this looks like it's got some serious security." He watched her insert access codes into a computer panel next to the front door, then unlock two dead bolts. Much barking ensued on the other side of the door. "You brought Eloise?"

"I dropped her off this morning along with some of my stuff. I usually stay here during the week to take care of family business and then head over to my apartment on the weekends to put it all behind me." She tugged open the heavy door and stepped inside, holding it wide for him. "Do you want to come in?"

Wes could practically smell the money drifting out of the place. From his glimpse of bronze antiques, leather bound books lining the hallway and a grand, sweeping staircase in the foyer behind her, he saw a much different side of Tempest. She could surround herself with soap operas and her statue-making hobby all she wanted, but she'd never be the anonymous downtown artist she tried to project in her Chelsea apartment.

Tempest Boucher had always been the favorite daughter of the social pages, a pampered heiress whose exclusive lifestyle he could view from afar but never truly join.

"No thanks." He'd only be more off his game if he stepped foot inside. "I just wanted to make sure you got home safe. I've got some work to do on the case."

"The murder?" She paused in the door, as if she dreaded entering the huge home as much as he did. Eloise stepped out over the threshold for a greeting, stationing her brown head under his hand just in case he wanted to pet her.

"I'm trying to line up some appointments for tomorrow to check out Blind Date." He scratched Eloise absently while he wondered if he'd be tangling the sheets with Tempest right now if they'd been able to go back to her apartment instead of here.

As she stood framed in the doorway, her luscious curves neatly outlined in her tailored suit, he remembered all the ways he still wanted her, all the things he hadn't tried with that scarf of hers yet. Their time together in her conference room hadn't been nearly enough to sate his appetite for this woman who confused him as much as she tempted him.

He was so caught up in thinking about what might have been, he somehow missed her scowling features. Her tense posture.

Her flat-out glare.

"You're still going on a date through MatingGame?" Her tone could freeze a man at twenty paces.

"It's a *job,* remember?" Damn it, they'd been over

this. "I still have to see if the Blind Date service is legit."

"Then by all means, Detective, go make your dates." She reached to pull the door shut between them, giving him a very literal cold shoulder. She would have slammed it in his face if he hadn't planted his foot in her way.

"Wait."

8

EVEN KNOWING she was being unreasonable, Tempest had no interest in whatever else Wes might have to say. Then again, she didn't want to break his foot. Easing off the door, she glared at him through the narrow opening.

"What?" She bit out the word with every ounce of hauteur she could scavenge because no way would she let him see that his decision to forge ahead with the dates actually stung where she was most vulnerable. Some wishful part of her brain had actually convinced her maybe he'd changed his mind about serial dating after the way they'd connected earlier.

She'd tried to give him his space after the conference table, but apparently he needed *way* more space than her sensibilities would allow. And so what if she was being unfair? She'd grown up chubby and graceless, the bane of her chic mother's existence. Although she'd conquered enough of her insecurities to be effective at her temporary CEO job and a damn good artist, she didn't have the kind of self-confidence required to be with a man whose job demanded he date women with sexually kinky tastes.

Especially not now, when her private haven and her lone claim to independence had been sniffed out by the media. Her apartment would be staked out by snap-happy photographers.

"I can't leave when you're mad at me." He shoved his hands in the pockets of his trench coat. "You know the only reason I'm setting up appointments with these women is to test out MatingGame. I would think you'd be glad to clear your company's name."

"Maybe I'm not upset on my business's behalf." She knew she was being irrational but couldn't seem to shake her frustration—which only made her angrier. She crossed her arms and continued to send out frosty vibes, a feat made difficult by Eloise's damned annoying tail-wagging attempts to shove her aside so she could get at Wes.

Traitorous animal.

"You're offended because…" He genuinely seemed clueless as he searched for the answer, his gray eyes narrowing. Behind him the rain kicked up again, sending pedestrian traffic scurrying for cabs and a nearby subway station. "You're jealous?"

"I am not jealous of a bunch of sex-starved strangers who will try to tear your clothes off the moment they see you." Damn the man. Did she have to spell it out for him? "I'm just not the kind of self-assured woman who can handle being with a guy who undertakes risque assignments after jumping my bones in my conference room a few hours ago. Does that make sense to you?"

He stared at her in calm silence, a frustrating response to angry feelings she didn't know quite where to put.

"You're the detective, Wes. I would think you'd be well-versed in drawing conclusions about people's motivations." She huffed out a sigh as she leaned into the doorjamb and tried to let it go. "I know I'm being way too uptight about the dating thing, I just—"

Don't want any one else to touch you.

Not sure how to complete the thought, she waited. Debated. And spied a photographer adjusting his camera lens no more than twenty yards away.

Crap.

"You'd better come inside." Reaching for Wes's sleeve, she tugged him closer. "There's a snoopy camera guy two doors down."

She had to admire that he didn't immediately swivel his head over to check it out for himself. That was most people's gut reaction and it made for the best full-face shots for press hounds.

"That's just as well." He plowed his way into the house, bolting the door behind him before he peered discreetly through the blinds on a nearby window. Turning to face her, jaw set, his eyes flashed with cool fire. "Because we need to talk, anyway."

"Oh." Thoughts of the invasive photographer fell by the wayside. She felt a bit like she'd baited a beast, egging on Wes until she'd fired him up, and now that she had him, she wasn't quite certain what to do with him. "I thought you had work to do?"

Too bad she couldn't work up the appropriate level of sarcasm since she was beginning to realize that any sensitivity she displayed on the subject only led Wes to believe she cared.

"Lucky for me, I can sign online to set up my work appointments anytime. But I'm not going to be able to get a damn thing done until we get a few things squared away."

His voice reverberated in the cavernous hall foyer, his words softly repeating themselves.

Nodding, she decided sparring with Wes got her nowhere. Better to hear him out and then figure out how to handle the tricky new twists to their relationship once his big, tempting body was out of sight.

And more importantly, out of reach.

"Can we go someplace a little less…echoing?" Gesturing to the twelve-foot ceilings and miles of mahogany wainscoting, he kept his eyes on her. "Your bedroom, maybe?"

"Don't you think that's a little presumptuous?"

"You said this house isn't you. I just want to go to whatever corner of the monolith you have carved out for yourself. If it's not a bedroom, maybe a sitting room?" He shook his head as his gaze scanned the rows of doors visible down the front corridor. "A library? Or do you have your own frigging parlor around here somewhere, Ms. Boucher?"

Sighing, she nodded toward the stairs. "I have the third floor actually. Come on."

She whistled to Eloise, who scampered in the back of the first floor where she liked to reign supreme over an outdoor courtyard. After settling the dog with a few Milk-Bones she'd stashed on the dining room table that morning, Tempest returned to face Wes, along with her fears of what she was getting herself into with him.

He followed her up the steps, a silent shadow near enough to send prickles of awareness through her. Hastening her pace as they reached her floor, she tried not to think about the way she'd given herself so completely into this man's hands today. She'd done such a good job maintaining boundaries with men, up until Wes, and now they were crumbling fast in spite of her good intentions.

She had made a deal with herself long ago that she'd rather be lonely now and hold out for a Grand Passion down the road. No sense having her somewhat tender heart trampled mercilessly until then. And since most men seemed more interested in her connections or her money, keeping her distance hadn't been all that difficult.

But this man had gotten under her skin from the moment he'd walked into her trashed apartment, asking questions, taking names and generally getting in her face. Now that she'd shared a piece of herself with him today, she found herself more attracted than ever, and disappointed with herself that she didn't possess the kind of confidence necessary to be okay with him dating other women all day.

Whatever happened to good, old-fashioned police interviews like they showed on *Law & Order?* Then again, Wes couldn't go that route since the dating service didn't give out any personal information about its clients.

"Here we are," she said finally, leading him into the living area outside her bedroom. Furnished with comfortable wingbacks and inviting ottomans, the room still contained a few of her mother's favorite paintings valued well over the cost of a new car, but at least there was nothing priceless and nothing too precious. Tempest had broken enough irreplaceable objects in her life for her parents to take her at her word when she said she didn't want anything too fussy up here.

"It's better." Wes made the pronouncement without even looking around. Tossing his trench coat aside, he took her hand. "Sit with me."

He tugged her down to a low ottoman covered in faux fur. Tempest had it made for her mother to rest her feet on since she had the beginnings of arthritis in both ankles, but Mom had thought it a little too plebian and chose to be sore rather than risk setting her toes on something unfashionable.

"Just for a minute." She didn't want Wes to think they were going to replay the scene in her conference room today. Not when he had a file folder full of other women he needed to date.

Argh. Did she *have* to keep thinking about that?

He laced his fingers together, hands clasped between sprawled knees as he faced her. "I didn't want to undergo the whole post-sex conversational dance at your office, but I think we made a mistake not talking about what happened today."

"I'm well aware what happened today." She tugged her skirt lower on her thighs, her body already tingling responsively at the man's proximity.

Obviously her body wasn't nearly as offended as her brain.

"I don't want it to be a one-time deal."

That caught her off guard. "But what about the media circus? You've already had a small taste, and it'll be worse tomorrow morning when you see the papers. Especially since they're already staking out my home. I can call some security to keep the worst of the press out of this neighborhood, but it won't be so easy to avoid them at my studio."

She hated the idea of her private sanctuary invaded by camera crews. Reporters seeking sensationalism over the facts.

"I'll tell the world I'm your bodyguard. Cops moonlight with stuff like that all the time." He shrugged it off like it was no big deal when she knew it would be. No man's ego would enjoy the inevitable innuendos that would wind up in the tabloids.

"So you're saying you want something more from this?" She swirled the air between them with her finger, referencing the connection she felt every time Wes got within arm's length.

"I don't know what I want exactly. But I know I'm not ready to let you go." He slid a hand beneath her hair, cupping her neck. His thumb stroked a path down the base of her skull while he ventured closer, devouring her with his gray gaze.

She found it difficult to unglue her tongue from the roof of her mouth, but she forced herself to speak before she lost herself in his hungry stare. If he could be honest with her, he deserved that much in return. "I know it's not fair to you, but I don't like to think about you dating women who will want you as badly as I do."

She was entitled to a few insecurities as long as she was up front about them, right?

"You just need to remember, I'm searching for a killer, not a sex partner." His voice whispered over her with a bracing reminder, igniting fresh fears in her already pounding heart. She didn't like to think about the risks inherent to his profession. In her world, the big danger was getting flayed by the press. In Wes's world, he put his life in peril on a regular basis.

Admiration stole through her along with the certainty she was being insecure. Overcautious.

Yet she had to admit it soothed her wounded ego that he wanted to see her again. How could she ever overcome her self-doubts if she didn't take a few risks?

Willing away her fears, she reached out to touch him.

"How about right now?" Laying her palm over his chest, she found his pulse beat out the same cagey rhythm as hers. The pounding calmed her at the same time it sent warm ripples of answering heat through her. "What are you searching for now that I've brought you deep into my lair, Detective?"

"I'm looking for the real Tempest Boucher." He smoothed a finger down the delicate column of her neck. "And I'm not leaving until I uncover every clue and explore every last inch."

His touch undid her. Made her forget any reason she might have had for caution.

Her eyes slid closed as she gave herself over to the pure pleasure of his hands on her skin. After a long draught of no sex in her life, her body ached for more of Wes. Their encounter on the conference table had merely whet her appetite.

He popped the buttons on her jacket, sending them bouncing to the hardwood floor like the first gentle drops of rain before the rush of a full-fledged storm.

Already the warning thunder rumbled through her nerves, rattling her thoughts and vibrating her most sensitive places. She threw her head back, giving him better access to her neck, her breasts…anywhere he wanted.

With Wes, she could almost allow herself to feel beautiful. Confident. Utterly alluring.

"Then I'm turning myself in for a thorough inspection."

HE COULD DO THOROUGH.

For this woman full of surprising contrasts, he thought he could damn near do anything. And *this?* She wanted all the same things he did.

Wes flicked her jacket off her arms, careful to leave the scarf dangling around her neck, skimming her breasts to taste more thoroughly now that they had time. Unhooking the clasp on her bra, he watched her curves spring free from their restraint, the taut peaks evident beneath the sheer barrier of her long scarf.

Sliding the silk fabric down her chest, he twined the material under her breasts until he cradled their weight in the soft fabric. Lifting them as he lowered his mouth to taste her, he rolled each nipple between his lips, sucking hard until she clawed at his shirt. His pants.

Her sensual hunger left him awed. When he first met her, there had seemed something sort of shy and reserved about Tempest, almost as if she wasn't completely comfortable in her pinup girl body. But once her clothes started coming off, she was a different woman, an uninhibited sex goddess ready to feed all her desires with him.

Only him.

Releasing the scarf, he undid a couple of shirt buttons and popped the rest, figuring if she could sacrifice her jacket he could damn well sacrifice his shirt. This was about getting naked, about seeing more of her than he'd seen in her conference room. He wanted to know her better, understand her more.

He couldn't imagine a woman who had so many things going for her harboring such deep-seated insecurities. Maybe he had more than enough ego for both of them, because some part of him kept insisting he could chase away her fears if only he had enough time to lavish every inch of her with his undivided attention.

His pants hit the floor in time with her skirt. She'd lost her panties to his appetite in her office, leaving her fully exposed, a decadent feast for the taking.

While he gawked like a teenager at the spectacular view, Tempest tugged down his shorts, availing herself of his cock. She smoothed her palm down his shaft, her creamy skin a wicked enticement. Circling the head with her thumb, she dropped to her knees in front of him. And then...

His brain short-circuited from the heat blasting through his veins. Her mouth closed over him, gently sucking, flicking her tongue all around the sensitive ridge of the head. She drew him in deeper and deeper, the wet warmth killing him until sweat popped out along his lip.

Two could play that game.

"Who's supposed to be doing the exploring today?" He drew her up by her elbows, desperate for her taste on his mouth. "Your turn to submit yourself to me."

Licking her lips as she got to her feet, she would have fallen if he hadn't laid her out on the oversize fur ottoman, her thighs dangling off the edge.

Perfect.

He settled himself between her legs, zeroing in on her clit. So much for taking his time. She'd gotten him hot so fast he couldn't think how to control himself or how to hold back. He only knew he needed the taste of her. Now.

Swirling his tongue deep in her slit he made love to her with his mouth the same way he'd make love to her with his cock soon enough. Right after she came for him.

Plucking at the center of her plump sex, he felt the throbbing heat of her pulse hard between her thighs. But still it wasn't enough. With his other hand he roamed her body, over her belly to cup her breast and tweak one tight nipple.

Her cry was his only warning before her body spasmed hard, clenching again and again while her skin suffused with heat. A beautiful sight.

He didn't let her go yet. Not until every last spasm had its way with her. Only then did he kiss her sex one last time and stretch out over top of her, covering her.

Blindly, he sought the condom he'd left near the ottoman where he'd discarded his pants. It rested by their feet now that they'd rolled the piece of furniture into the sofa with their frantic movements. Wes spun them back near the condom so he could protect her, making sure he brought this woman only pleasure.

"Please. Let me." She took the packet from his hands, her movements faster but not necessarily more efficient. Her hand shook ever so slightly, her body practically humming with sexual energy.

That quiver of hers humbled him, reminding him how damn lucky he was to touch her right now. He watched her as she peeled the condom down his shaft, then lined up his cock with her slick passage. He was more than ready.

His hips thrust gently at first, allowing her to get used to him. She clawed at his back, her short nails a welcome counterpoint to the mind-drugging pleasure of her soft form beneath him, her wet heat clinging all around him.

Driving deeper, he relished the way her hands moved over his chest, then over her own chest. She plucked at her nipple, teasing the tight peak with one finger until she saw him watching. Smiling, she reached up to his mouth to wet two digits and used the dampness to trace a wet circle around one rosy crest.

She made him crazy.

Out of his mind, past obsession-crazy. And with that thought in mind, his gaze glued to the sweet temptation of one nipple, he thrust hard inside her once, twice...

They came together in a rush of harsh cries and ragged moans. Her feet pinned the backs of his thighs down, as if to keep him inside her forever. Her hips arched up against his in the most intimate of matings, her heat pressed tightly to him.

He didn't know what his thorough inspection of Tempest had uncovered about her, but he knew a hell of a lot more about himself for his efforts.

For starters, he now realized he didn't have any idea how he would ever walk away from this woman once the threat that stalked her had been caught.

THE PARK AVENUE mausoleum echoed and creaked after Wes's departure, amplifying Tempest's sense of loss. Running her palm over the still-warm sheet where he'd laid beside her until a few minutes ago, she breathed in his scent—their scent—until she could almost feel his strong, solid presence beside her again.

Foolish, romantic notion.

She wished she could be the kind of woman who boldly conducted affairs with men, taking the sex and fun, then walking away with heart intact. But she'd been a Sap with a capital S since childhood, surrounding herself in rainbows and unicorns, dotting her very first letter "i" with a heart.

Her fast-living parents had no idea where she

came by her love for happy endings. Their own marriage had been a study in dysfunction since her ambitious, east Texas father wed Solange, Tempest's old-money mother, for her family's Louisiana gambling connections. The two of them had plotted and schemed their way into the highest echelons of New York society with their combined drive and Ray's knack for making money, their marriage falling apart once they'd both achieved their material dreams.

They had both looked upon their daughter's tender heart with pity, encouraging her to think big and use her privileges in life to expand the family empire rather than offering leftover meals to homeless people.

So it hardly came as a surprise to Tempest that she was already weaving romantic dreams around Wes Shaw. How could she expect anything less of herself when the man had given her more orgasms in an evening than she'd had in the last three years combined? Of course she was feeling a little bit vulnerable tonight.

And it didn't help to be here, in the empty home of her past where she would never fulfill her childhood dream of seeing her parents happy together, their family whole.

She simply needed to acknowledge her foolish, romantic weaknesses and get over them. Her mother was happy enough being the toast of London society, and her dad had chosen to live his life to the extreme, right up until his last breath. No childish fancies on Tempest's part would change that.

And for his part, Wes would go out with half of

the New York–based women using the Blind Date service of MatingGame, so apparently he wasn't nursing any romantic feelings about her in return.

Tempest would get her butt out of bed and the stars out of her eyes before she started pinning any personal hopes on Wes. He'd gone above and beyond professional duty to keep her safe and catch the person responsible for breaking into her apartment. The least she could do for him in return was keep her heart on a leash and pay attention to his ongoing investigation.

Lowering her feet to the floor, she levered herself up and out of bed, dragging the sheet along with her as she sought the laptop in her overnight bag.

Maybe she'd go surf the MatingGame site again just in case she came up with something new, some hint of what really went on at the small company she'd once envisioned as a romantic new way for couples to find each other. Of course, if she'd been completely honest she'd have to admit some perverse part of her also wanted to read the profiles posted on the site and guess which ones had intrigued Wes enough to ask them out.

Switching on a lamp at the scroll-top desk across the room, Tempest flipped the soft bed linens over her shoulder, toga-style. She opened one screen after another on the Web site, hoping to find any clue Wes might have overlooked. Her phone call to the operations manager of the site had gone unanswered since Saturday, but in the woman's defense, she had planned to be away for a few days on personal business.

Then again, what if that business involved leaving town for good? Could she have been aware of misconduct in the company and skipped out before her role was uncovered?

Tempest found it hard to believe that scenario, but given her tendency to see the world through rose-colored glasses, she could hardly trust her own judgment.

That applied double with Wes, damn it.

Punching the keys that took her to her own profile on the Blind Date portion of the site, Tempest reread the words she'd written about herself even though she knew she couldn't go out on a date with a stranger when the only man who interested her at the moment was Wes. To her surprise, there were over one thousand page views on her profile, along with a private message at the top of her screen alerting her that she had mail waiting in her MatingGame account.

Curious, she clicked through the sign-in steps to access the inbox and discovered thirty-two e-mails with subject headers ranging from "Best ride of your life—guaranteed" to "Ever had twelve inches?"

Assured that this was *not* the way a self-described sap would ever meet a man, Tempest nearly clicked the screen closed when an e-mail ID jumped out at her.

KingKong.

It took her a moment to make the connection and recall why it seemed familiar. Wes had named his dog Kong.

Fingers propelled by a rush of curiosity, she

clicked on KingKong's subject header that read simply, "Meet Me?" Probably just a coincidence. Then again, Wes said he'd tried to line up a few dates.

Why should her heart speed up at the thought of Wes choosing her anonymous profile when he'd told her ten times his dates were strictly business?

The letter opened, taking up the width of her screen with white space except for a few simple lines—"I'd like to get to know you better and I'm willing to pick up the tab. Meet you at Mick's Grill on the lower West side tomorrow at 8:00 p.m.?"

The note wasn't signed, but included a link to a profile on the site. A click of the mouse led her to the familiar profile she'd watched Wes create to lure potential prostitutes.

He'd chosen her. Whether he had simply arranged as many dates as possible or he'd spied something interesting in her profile remained to be seen.

Eloise whimpered at her feet and crawled closer to Tempest for an ear scratch.

Sighing, she patted her dog absently. "I know, I know. He's looking for a woman who turns tricks for a living, so why should I be flattered, right?"

Still, she'd be lying if she said the note from KingKong didn't lift her spirits. Maybe it was because the communication helped prove her theory that MatingGame provided a legitimate service. Or possibly the warm sense of satisfaction inside her stemmed from the fact that she'd found a way to wrangle a second date with the sexiest man she'd ever met.

But Tempest feared her sudden surge of optimism

didn't really relate to either of those things. Ridiculous though it might be, she celebrated her small victory tonight because she hadn't included anything remotely sexual in her profile on Blind Date and Wes had said he'd be on the lookout for profiles openly offering explicit sex.

Her profile had none.

Coincidence? Not in her romantic heart, it wasn't. Detective Wesley Shaw might have been working when he'd chosen to set up dates with the other women on his list, but some deep-seated feminine instinct told her he wanted to meet her for more personal reasons.

And there wasn't a chance she would disappoint her blind date.

9

"YOU DISAPPOINT ME, Shaw." Vanessa Torres knotted her long, dark hair into a braid while she squinted down at the morning paper spread out over her desk at the precinct. "You finally made the social pages and you couldn't even trouble yourself to shine your shoes? The trench coat is pretty stylin' though. Maybe there's hope for you yet."

Stationed at the desk beside her, Wes ignored his partner the same way he'd blown off the landslide of jabs from his colleagues, including a life-size blow-up of the newspaper photo some wiseass glued to a piece of cardboard and posted in the break room. The homemade artwork wouldn't have been so bad except that the joker responsible had carefully colored a border of pansies around the photo.

He could take a lot of crap, but any guy who implied he was a pansy had a serious ass-kicking coming to him.

Vanessa chattered on, unruffled by his silence. "So Tempest Boucher is the new Flavor of the Month? It's good to see you getting back in the game, but high-class chicks like this might not appreciate the old Wes Shaw cut-and-run routine four weeks from now."

That got his attention.

Wes spun away from his computer, where he'd been coordinating a dating schedule that would put the world's biggest Casanovas to shame.

"Has it ever occurred to you, Torres, that maybe *I'm* not the one who does the cutting and running after a month?"

Vanessa leaned back in her chair, her sleek leather jacket rustling with the movement. A five-year member of the force, she still seemed like a rookie. Not that she didn't do her job well. On the contrary, Wes had seen this five-foot-eight, trim woman collar some seriously big guys when push came to shove. But she remained a loner in a job that necessitated strong partnerships, preferring to maintain strict privacy about her personal life and never allowing anyone to get too close to her.

A few guys on the male-dominated force had tried to write her off as an ice princess, but Wes defended her whenever the insults got any worse than that. He didn't know what made Vanessa so aloof with most of the guys, but he understood the need to be left alone better than most. Maybe that's why they made good partners. They might share cases, but they were each content to operate solo for the better part of every day.

"That's an interesting scenario." Vanessa tapped her chin as if deep in thought, but a telltale crease in her cheek—an optimistic dimple in a cynical face— assured Wes she still messing with him. "You think you possess some sort of time-release scariness that makes women from all walks of life begin to see your true nature after exactly four weeks and decide to give you the old heave-ho?"

"I've had relationships last longer than four weeks." He didn't know why he bothered to hand over that piece of information now, when he had never felt compelled to share as much with her any other time she'd hassled him.

Maybe it was because he couldn't envision getting his fill of Tempest in a few weeks' time. The woman appealed to him on an instinctual level even though their being together made no sense from a logical standpoint.

"You?" Vanessa tipped forward in the ancient wooden office chair, the hardware squawking with the movement. "The king of love 'em and leave 'em? I've been with the NYPD for five years, Romeo, even if I've only been your partner for the past eighteen months. Don't try to tell me you've hooked up with anyone serious in all that time."

"It so happens I haven't, since my stints at longterm predated your arrival." He'd been burning a path through girlfriends in the couple of years before his first partner died—a knee-jerk reaction to two previous relationships where he'd been played. "But what makes you think you knew anything about me from the days before you got assigned to hold my hand and make sure I didn't go off the deep end after Steve went missing?"

He understood that had been a small part of Vanessa's job back then—keep an eye on Wes and make sure he handled the guilt. Wes had blamed himself for not taking a bigger role in Steve's undercover assignment, for not seeing warning signs that he was getting in too fast, too far.

And then once he'd turned up dead, Wes couldn't deceive himself any longer that his friend had slipped into deep cover somewhere to make a big bust or bring down a whole crime syndicate. Wes had never been much for wishful thinking, but coming up with possible scenarios to explain Steve's disappearance had kept him from facing the final truth for over a year.

"Honestly?" Vanessa folded up her newspaper and chucked it in the wastebasket along with Wes's social page debut. "I had the hots for you when I first came on board here."

Wes had never been a man of excess words, and he couldn't have come up with a response to that one if his life depended on it.

"No need to look so terrified, Clouseau." She whipped him on the arm with a pencil. "I'm long over any feeling of attraction for a guy who sucks at relationships even worse than I do."

Relief smacked him like a tidal wave. Vanessa was nice enough, and he admired her skills as a top-notch cop, but she seemed way too complicated. And although she was Bronx born and bred, something about her still screamed high-maintenance.

Funny that Tempest was about as uptown as a woman could get, yet she didn't strike Wes as high-maintenance at all. Somehow a woman with dog hair on her suits who called microwave popcorn a meal seemed more like his type.

"I've seen that Ginsu crap you do. I could never

date a woman who kicks more ass than me." He planned on keeping his head permanently attached to his shoulders, thank you very much.

"It's kendo. Ginsu makes knives." She rolled her eyes. "I guess I just thought—at first glance—that you and I were kind of alike. A couple of loners in the midst of the big cop family where everyone knows everyone else's business. I didn't realize back then you were so much a loner that you were completely relationship challenged."

"Guilty." He could hardly deny the obvious. Thinking he'd reached his quota on personal chat for the day, Wes turned back to his computer to finish logging in his appointments for the afternoon and evening.

"You know, if you decide you want this Tempest woman to stick around longer than four weeks, it couldn't hurt to try trusting her a little." Vanessa pulled a red floral day planner out of a desk drawer and dumped it in her purse. "No one appreciates it when you expect the worst from them."

"Trust is something earned, not given." He'd learned that the hard way with women. Twice. And even then he'd told himself he could at least trust his partner, a mistake he wouldn't make again with Vanessa even though they got along just fine. But he'd thought Steve was his friend and the guy either sold out to the lure of money or he'd simply gotten way too careless on a job where every breath he took should have been weighed and measured.

Shoving herself to her feet, Vanessa breezed past him, the leather strap of her jacket's belt slapping the back of his chair. "You keep telling yourself that, Wes. I'm sure it will be comforting next month when your uptown girl dumps you." She paused to fill a cup of water from the cooler on her way to the door. "Just don't forget people are very good at living up to your worst expectations. It's a satisfying fact of the cynic's creed."

She lifted her cup of water toward him in a mock toast and then sailed out of the room before Wes realized he hadn't told her squat about his progress on the case.

Damn.

So maybe Vanessa had a valid point about him being a loner. And a tad cynical. That didn't mean he couldn't keep Tempest in his life longer than a month if he wanted.

Although, as he stared unseeing at his computer screen with the list of women he planned to meet starting this afternoon at one o'clock, he had to admit he was already well on his way to pissing her off. She hadn't liked him arranging dates as part of his investigation, but he'd went ahead and made the arrangements anyway since Tempest hadn't been able to produce the woman at MatingGame who should have the answers to his questions.

The appointments were the only way to find out more about the women who used the Blind Date service. Forcing thoughts of Tempest from his mind, Wes returned to his private message box at the MatingGame site and found two more responses to his e-mails requesting dates. Guilt nipped him as he realized that one of the notes came from a woman whose profile had caught his eye on a personal level. He'd streamlined his investigation to include only women who posted blatantly sexual profiles on the Web site—except for one that snagged his eye because he'd been thinking about Tempest.

He nearly deleted the post, knowing his dates didn't have a damn thing to do with his personal life, but at the last minute he paused. Thought about it.

Maybe he should meet one woman who hadn't mentioned a lot of kinky sex anyhow, sort of like a standard for comparison in a science experiment. His 8:00 p.m. meeting with the dog owner who described her ideal foreplay as a good conversation would give him a more rounded look at Blind Date's clientele anyway, something Tempest's company deserved.

Confirming the time and place with the last woman on his list via e-mail through Blind Date's private account, Wes had every intention of catching his criminal this week. His time frame for solving the case seemed all the more urgent after Tempest's apartment had been trashed. What if she was next on the killer's list? While he couldn't be sure the break-in had been related to last week's murder, he knew he'd sleep a hell of a lot better once the person responsible had been caught.

Maybe then he'd be able to figure out how to convince Tempest to stick around for more than a few weeks. Because, no matter what Vanessa said about his ability to trust, Tempest was one woman he didn't have any intention of letting go.

TONIGHT SHE WOULD LET GO of all her inhibitions.

Tempest had told herself as much ten times over on the cab ride to Mick's Grill in the lower West side. But while banishing her inhibitions in the bedroom sounded easy enough, she hadn't fully prepared herself for the challenge of being loose and carefree on the streets of New York at night.

And not just loose in a figurative sense. No, Tempest had elected to wear the trench coat Wes left at her place and nothing more for her rendezvous tonight, so her breasts were jiggling around inside the jacket like mounds of unconfined Jell-O.

What had she been thinking?

Her gaze skated up to meet the cabby's eyes in the rearview mirror, hoping he hadn't noticed any unusual breast activity. Luckily he was flipping off the guy in the taxi behind him, completely engaged in his work.

God bless the high level of job commitment in New York cabdrivers.

Swallowing back an attack of nerves, Tempest figured as long as she could pay the man his fare and get out of the car without giving anyone on the street an eyeful of cellulite, she'd be okay. Once she had Wes in her sights again, she would focus only on their night together—the night she planned to shed the last of her hang-ups and concentrate solely on pleasure. After all, she'd progressed beyond the blindfold stage and was now well on her way to making serious strides in the bold and brazen department.

Nervous and a little excited, she tipped the cabby

and stepped out of the car with extreme caution. Awareness of her nudity beneath the coat made everything about her surroundings feel sexual. The rumble of a truck vibrated through her as it hurried down the street. The hiss of steam from a subway vent snaked up her thighs to warm her intimately. At the corner, the stoplight turned from yellow to red, bathing a handful of pedestrians in a seductive flush of color.

Amazing how the simple absence of undies filtered all her perceptions through a sex lens.

Tugging on the ends of the coat's belt, she made sure she was still covered before pulling open the door to Mick's Grill. An old Billy Joel tune spilled out onto the street along with scents of spicy teriyaki sauce. The small bar and eatery wasn't jam-packed, but it seemed crowded for a Tuesday night.

Weaving her way past the corporate crowd that liked to invade the quirky establishments on the lower West side in a relentless search for atmosphere, Tempest spied more room in the back where the locals congregated. Squinting through the hazy smoke from the grill, she thought she spied her personal KingKong at the back corner table where he said he'd be. But wasn't that a woman just leaving his booth?

Irritated, she would have stomped straight over to her date's female companion to claim Wesley Shaw for her own, but something about the woman's familiar posture stopped her.

Tall and slim, the redhead possessed a confident stance as she bent to place a flirtatious kiss on Wes's cheek. Her dress was short and sexy, designed to catch a man's eye.

Recognition came when the woman turned on one red-and-white polka-dot heel.

Kelly Kline, Boucher's vice president of global development.

Flustered and not sure what else to do, Tempest darted closer to the bar, ducking under the arm of a short guy in a suit so Kelly wouldn't see her.

"Well, *hello*." The balding Mr. Corporate huffed a beer-stinking breath over her before he nearly fell face-first into her exposed cleavage.

Eyes glued on Kelly's disappearing red dress, Tempest shoved away from the barfly and scrambled closer to Wes, concerned that maybe they'd overlooked something by not examining her work associates sooner. Could Kelly have trashed her apartment in anger? If office gossip held true, the woman probably harbored a fair share of anger with Tempest for not giving her a chance at the CEO slot.

Coincidence that she'd shown up here tonight? Tempest didn't think her driven business associate was capable of murder, but it didn't sit well to see the woman among Wes's suspects when she already had reason to resent Tempest.

Picking up the pace, she reached Wes in a distracted huff, eager to share her suspicions.

"I know that woman." She began without prelude as she latched on to Wes's arm, pointing toward the front of the bar where Boucher's most ambitious employee had vanished.

"What the hell are you doing here?" Wes slid out

of the rounded corner booth to stand, rapidly insert-ing himself between her and the crush of the dinner crowd and assorted happy hour partygoers. "I'm in-terviewing suspects, damn it."

"I know. I just wanted to—" It was rather compli-cated actually. She hadn't planned to greet him so abruptly.

What's more, he looked less than pleased and maybe even a little suspicious.

"How did you even know where to find me?" Frowning, he nudged her toward the curved bench seat and settled across from her at the table.

"You asked me to meet you." She hoped he wasn't going to be mad about this. But damn it, she had a right to be here to prove to him Blind Date had set them up legitimately. "I'm the dog owner whose ideal foreplay is good conversation."

"You?" Wes looked confused for about a nanosecond before a small tic started pulsing be-neath his left eye. "You entered your profile on Blind Date?"

"I figured if you were trying it out to see how it worked, I could, too." She didn't mention that she'd also toyed with the idea of trying to date her way out of her fixation with him. The tic under his eye warned her this was really *not* the time to bring it up. "Once I saw a note from KingKong, I remembered about your dog and I knew it was you, so—"

"I'm a trained investigator looking for a killer and I happen to be armed for the job." The tic picked up speed. "You care to tell me what makes *you* qual-ified to test the system, Nancy Drew?"

Okay, now that pissed her off.

"I own the company, Wes. This might be just another case to you, but Boucher Enterprises is my whole life. I'm not going to sit back and watch it go belly-up because of some deranged prostitute on a killing spree."

A harried-looking waiter arrived before Wes could say anything. The college kid with a crooked bowtie picked up a leftover glass with a red lipstick print on the rim and asked Tempest what she wanted.

"No, thanks, we were just leaving," Wes informed him, tossing a wad of cash on the guy's tray.

"I'll have a vodka tonic with a twist, no ice." Tempest never took her gaze off Wes, refusing to be steamrolled.

As the waiter took off, she leaned forward over the table, needing to clarify one more point. "And furthermore, I don't even think you're right about the whole prostitution angle. The woman you were meeting before me happens to be an employee of my company and trust me, we keep her *far* too busy for her to moonlight as a hooker. She also happens to make plenty of money by using her brain, without having to throw her body into the mix."

"You mean Katrina?" Wes's gaze flicked down to Tempest's breasts, lingering long enough to send a rush of heat through her. By the time he met her eyes again, the tic had faded. "She also happens to have damn kinky tastes."

"Well her name isn't Katrina, it's Kelly Kline and although I can't picture her having any reason to murder a man she met through the MatingGame site, she does have reason to be unhappy with me since I'm the biggest obstacle to her stepping into the CEO shoes at Boucher."

"You think she might have been the person who trashed your apartment?" Wes lifted a skeptical brow as he straightened his skinny silk tie. Between the retro neckwear and a slightly faded pinstripe suit, he looked like a gangster from the forties. All he needed was the fedora.

"I don't know. I just thought it seemed odd that you're here looking for a killer and possibly someone who's upset with me because I'm in the wrong business, and in walks Kelly." She smiled up at the waiter as her vodka tonic arrived. "Thank you."

"I see you brought my coat back." Wes's eyes drifted lazily over her after the waiter left.

Music pulsed through the bar, the light rock changing to old seventies disco tunes. And thanks to a Gloria Gaynor song, Tempest began to feel very bold and brazen as "I Will Survive" blasted over the speakers.

"I did." She smoothed her hands over the lapels and admired the texture of the finely woven garment. "Although I like it so much, I think you're going to have to take it off me yourself if you want to get it back."

His focus narrowed solely to her, his nostrils flaring as he stared at her across the table. "I'm not willing to part with the coat."

She sipped the vodka, allowing the alcohol to tingle pleasantly through her veins and enhance the buzz of sexual awareness humming through her.

"Really? Then why don't we take this in the alley and you can fight me for it?"

Wes reached over the table, suddenly very interested in the coat. He slid a finger under the lapel of the jacket and skimmed it down. Down.

His gray eyes darkened, stormy and foreboding. "Just what the hell do you have on under there?"

SHE COULDN'T be naked.

No. Way. In. Hell. Yet even before her lips curled upward in a wicked grin, Wes knew the truth. The woman didn't have a stitch of clothing on beneath her trench coat. *His* coat, damn it. The same one he'd slung around his shoulders countless times now hugged her nude body, the silky lining caressing her skin the way he wanted to.

"I had the advantage of knowing who I was meeting for my blind date tonight, so I thought I'd dress accordingly." Her voice curled around him like a wisp of smoke from the fat candle flickering on their table.

"How do you know I don't have five other women lined up after you tonight?" He was still frustrated she'd shown up in the middle of his investigative work. What if she'd arrived during an arrest? Or worse, what if she'd gotten caught in a shoot-out with a desperate criminal?

She should have been a hell of a lot more careful. And he shouldn't be contemplating forgetting the lecture she deserved in favor of tearing the coat from her body.

"Do you?" She straightened, her abrupt attention

to posture robbing him of the delectable view he'd had down her jacket. "Have five other women lined up to meet you, I mean?"

Peering around the bar she nibbled on her bottom lip and looked unsettled. Worried.

Amazing how that small display of uncertainty could go so far toward evening the balance between them. He hadn't appreciated being caught off guard tonight.

"No." He finished her drink for her, the only sip of alcohol he'd allowed himself in eight hours at a bar. "Somehow I knew to save the best for last."

"So you did choose my profile for personal reasons." She reached under the table to put a hand on his thigh.

Her touch hadn't been the only occasion he'd been groped in his day of nonstop dating, but it was the first time he had enjoyed a feminine hand on his thigh. He pictured those neatly manicured nails clawing hungrily at his skin, her high society facade stripped away so that the real Tempest could have her way with him.

"I thought I should meet with one woman who hadn't blatantly advertised sex in her profile, just in case subversive hookers were more discreet than I thought." He found it difficult to converse with her in a noisy, public place when the only thought in his head right now was how fast he could have that coat off her.

"That's the only reason you picked me?" She slid closer to him in the rounded corner booth, giving herself all the more access to him under the table.

Her nails sketched higher on his thigh, lightly grazing his trousers and hovering to one side of his Johnson. "I was your control group?"

"We need to go." He reached beneath the table to imprison her wrist, thinking there was nothing "controlled" about the chemistry between them.

"What about my foreplay?" She wriggled her arm against his grip.

"You'll have all the time in the world to try out your moves as soon as I get you out of the coat." It was all he could think about. Her full breasts even moved differently underneath the fabric. In fact, now that he had realized she was naked, he was certain anyone who looked at her would notice right away.

"Not foreplay for you." She crossed her legs, rubbing one calf seductively against him. "I mean what about our good conversation? The foreplay for *me?*"

Tossing some bills on the table to settle their tab, Wes tugged Tempest out of the booth. "You should have thought of that before you went commando on me."

"Wait a minute—"

Her words were lost in the din of shouted conversations above the blaring disco music.

Wes kept his eye on the door and his arm around Tempest, determined no man in her path would get a bonus feel of anything save her elbow as she moved through the crowd. When he finally reached the door, he plowed through it so hard the metal barricade bounced back on the hinges against the building.

Fresh, rain-scented air blew over him, a welcome

relief after the muggy heat of the bar, but it didn't do a damn thing to cool the fire within. Drawing Tempest toward the alleyway between Mick's Grill and the laundromat next door, he figured he'd found the fastest path to a little privacy.

Ducking deeper into the shadows, Wes backed her against the brick wall of the building and reached for the tie of her coat.

"If you need a conversation first, you'd better start talking because we've got about five seconds before you're giving me one hell of a show."

10

"I'M AFRAID YOU'VE SEEN it all before, Detective." Tempest shifted on her skinny stilettos, the back of her heel scraping against the rough brick in the darkness. A streetlight shone a few yards away, near the curb, but their alleyway retreat remained shrouded in the comfort of anonymity. "Nothing new to show you tonight."

She loved how dangerous he looked in the shadows, his tall, lean outline tense with restrained hunger.

Loved?

Catching herself romanticizing, she wanted to correct herself but found she'd chosen the best word possible. Still, she could love something *about* the man without falling for him, right?

"On second thought—" growling low in his throat, Wes reached for the knotted belt at her waist, his finger tugging the fabric apart "—you've lost your conversational window, Tempest. Less talk, more nakedness."

A fluttery sensation tickled over her skin as she contemplated baring herself to him here. Now. Glancing sideways toward the street she didn't see anyone nearby. And Wes's big body would shield her from public view anyway.

She couldn't think of anything she wanted more right now than to expose herself to this man's hot gaze. Heat bubbled deep inside her and she welcomed the chance to bury old insecurities and fears forever. She thought she'd been finding herself by buying a downtown studio and defiantly watching soap operas before she threw herself into her artwork every weekend?

Ha! Wes Shaw was artwork in motion.

With him, she lived her hopes and dreams instead of imagining a world she'd never touched before. This moment with Wes was the real deal—the heat, the hunger, the wanting. She needed him so badly she could taste him even before he kissed her.

As the knot on her coat loosened, she pressed herself against the wall, fingers gripping along a mortar seam between bricks. She had to hold on to something before her trembling legs gave way beneath her.

When the belt slipped free completely, the coat hung around her, slightly parted but not enough that he would see anything in the shadows. A thin slice of cool night air drifted through that opening, heightening her anticipation.

"I'm waiting." Hardly daring to breathe in the tension-fogged air between them, Tempest bent one knee slightly and nudged a bare leg through the open slit. Her calf caught a shaft of light filtering into the alley from the streetlamp, her skin pale and luminous in the surrounding darkness.

Wes's hands plunged through the coat all at once, finding her belly and smoothing up, down, palming a breast at the same time he curved a hand around her hip. Releasing her hold on the wall, she twined her arms around his neck, falling into the hard planes of his body. His heat seared her, igniting a forbidden sizzle. Her breasts molded to him, heart beating so hard she could swear it pounded directly on his chest.

The coat cloaked her back and sides, even as it completely exposed her front. The full drape of the garment under her arms made her feel like a bat creature, a naughty, naked vampire on the loose.

For good measure, she shoved aside his jacket and nipped Wes's shoulder through his shirt, sinking her teeth lightly into his hot skin.

His touch grew rougher, more insistent, fingers sliding over the curve of her bottom to lift her against him. The delicious friction against her most tender parts only made her crave more of his wicked touch. Her moan echoed in the narrow alleyway before drowning in the honk of a cab out on the street.

A new fervor swirled low within her until her thighs twitched. She reached for his hand, determined to place his fingers where she needed them most.

His groan made her pause, her ragged breathing loud in her own ears.

"What?"

He stared down at her with enough blaze in his eyes to scorch her before he blinked slowly, deliberately, until some of that fire was banked. Marginally controlled.

"We've got to get out of here." Wes tried to edge away but her arms refused to release him.

"We only just got here." She gave a little shimmy, rolling her hips against his in an unmistakable message. "Besides, I'm the woman who won you fair and square from all the other females swarming around you today. I think I deserve my prize, KingKong."

Stroking her tongue up his jaw, she tugged at his tie, ready for more of him. She had no idea where this week's unexpected sexfest with him was going, but she didn't want it to end yet. He'd touched off some hunger within she hadn't known she possessed and now that the yawning ache had been unleashed, she knew he was the only man capable of fulfilling her.

She'd seen her parents be selfish all their lives, putting their own needs above their marriage. Above her. When would it be her turn to indulge in what she wanted? Just this once—for a few more days, a few more weeks—she planned to live like a hedonist and soak up every sensual touch of Wes Shaw's very capable hands. He would be her private indulgence.

"We can't risk it." His words confused her, but she wouldn't have stopped touching him until he backed away again—farther this time. "Someone might see us and if anyone recognizes you…"

He didn't need to complete the thought since she knew too well how devastating a naked tryst in the alley would be for her family's business. She damned his practicality even as she appreciated the cool head.

So much for her attempts to be selfish.

"You're right." To her horror, her voice broke. Oh God, she couldn't be that upset about delayed completion, could she? Obviously her emotions had gotten all tangled up where Wes was concerned despite her best efforts. Hoping to hide her slip, she reached for the belt on her coat, covering her gaffe with a flurry of sudden activity. "We can go to my house, if you want. The new security system is already in place at the Chelsea apartment."

He was so quiet, so still, she realized how presumptuous—and eager—she sounded. He peered down at her with an inscrutable expression on his face, studying her carefully.

Coat secured around her waist, she blasted forward toward the street, more determined than ever not to romanticize her time with Wes. She had vowed to take control of her own life as one of her New Year's resolutions, and this would be a fine time to prove to herself she didn't need anyone. "Then again you probably have things to do and that's fine, too. I should grab a cab and call it a night."

Wes caught her before she emerged into the light.

"I want to be with you." His words whispered over her ear with unexpected warmth, igniting shivery tingles down her neck until her skin tightened.

Relief, hope, anticipation—too many emotions scrambled inside her, making her aware of how much power she'd given him over her. Bad decision, Tempest. A woman didn't find emotional security and independence by making herself sexually reliant on a way-too-sexy detective.

As long as she kept it short-term, she could handle it. Heaven knew she would have traded her shares in Boucher Enterprises to have her cake and eat it, too, when it came to Wes.

"You do?" She closed her eyes for just a moment, soaking in the musky scent of his aftershave and the sharp cut of his angled jaw against her cheek.

"Trust me, I would have never risked my badge and your public image to cop a feel in an alley if you didn't make me crazy." He squeezed her tighter against him, allowing her to experience exactly how crazy she made him. The proof nudged insistently against her bottom.

"I never thought about the risk to your career." She stiffened in his grasp, uncomfortable with the idea of putting him in danger because of her newfound lust.

"It probably wouldn't have been a big deal, but when a detective is tapped for any kind of misbe-havior, the department becomes very unhappy." He threaded his fingers through her hair and tipped her head back, exposing her neck for a kiss. "We shouldn't let the nudity go public again."

Eyes sliding closed at the lash of his tongue on her throat, Tempest nodded. She could be indulgent. Selfish. Take what Wes had to offer for a little longer before she morphed into the independent super-woman of her New Year's goals.

"Got it. Private shows only. Now what do you say, Detective, your place or mine?"

MINE.

Wes had to continually hold himself back from speaking the word aloud when he was around this woman because he wanted to wrap her up and take her home, shield her from the eyes of the rest of the world so he could keep her for his alone.

A healthy, normal male desire?

Hell, no. He'd never been so possessive with any female in his life. And he had the misfortune of two notably bad relationships to teach him that no person can ever truly belong to another. So this caveman urge he battled around Tempest was stupid. Primitive.

Undeniable.

"Let's go to yours." He forced himself to articulate his choice very clearly, concentrating hard on not giving in to the urge to haul her back to his place. Hers would be safer, less intimate. "I can give the new security system the once-over."

"As long as *I* get more than a once-over." Her white teeth flashed in the shadows as she smiled.

"I can assure you more than once. But keep in mind I'm not one of these mythical soap opera studs who can go nonstop all night and then shower you with rose petals in the morning." Releasing her from his hold, he drew her out of the alley and into the street, relieved to see no reporters, no cameras.

"That's okay. I'm not much for rose petals anyway, since Eloise is allergic to flowers." She hugged her arms around her waist, her brown curls skimming the collar of her coat. "Why don't you just do what you can for me tonight, and we'll call it even?"

"Your dog has allergies?" Grateful for the reprieve from talking about sex when he wasn't free to act on it, Wes hailed a cab at the street corner.

"She's a very unique animal." Tempest fluffed

her hair and slid into the taxi, her long, bare legs giving him a view he wouldn't soon forget.

Seating himself beside her, Wes gave the driver the address of the Chelsea apartment a few blocks away. He'd walked to Mick's Grill from the precinct earlier, leaving the car for Vanessa to use. Now, settling inside the darkened interior, he fought to keep his hands off Tempest.

Because the next time he touched her, he wouldn't stop until he'd gotten his fill. He didn't know how she'd wound herself up in his thoughts so thoroughly that he could barely escape, but maybe once he'd caught whoever trashed her apartment, he'd be able to find his footing alone again.

Not exactly an inspiring thought, but Vanessa had nailed it on the head when she accused him of being too cynical to forge any kind of relationship these days. He didn't possess the kind of trust necessary to play much of a role in Tempest's life.

Hell, he didn't know if he even possessed enough trust to make a good partner for Vanessa. Not that she ever complained. But she damn well deserved someone to watch her back more than Wes had for the past year and a half.

That was going to change. He might not ever be the marrying kind, but he could damn well get his head out of his ass long enough to be a solid partner and an even better cop again. Spending time with Tempest had made him see how antisocial he'd become in the past two years and recognize that he didn't want to tread any further down that path.

As the cab rolled to a stop up the street from Tempest's building, she pulled out her wallet, offending him to his caveman core.

"You're money's no good with me." He paid the driver and helped her from the car while scowling at a handful of photographers who lurked around the doors to her building a few doors up.

"But you bought my drink." She still waved her wallet around like a magic wand to soothe over life's rough spots. She hadn't noticed the looming members of the media—yet. "It's only fair I get the cab. I don't want you to think I'm a moocher."

Grateful the cab hadn't let them out under a streetlight, Wes tucked her under his arm and pulled the collar of her trench coat up high around the lower part of her face.

"Who do you think has to worry more about mooching in this relationship? Me or you?" He plucked the pink leather zipper pouch from her fingers and jammed it back into a staid brown purse. Just like Tempest, her bag looked no-nonsense at a quick glance and hid a softer inside. "Besides, I'm a single cop whose only real bill to pay has been a hefty dog food tab. I think I can afford to keep you in vodka tonics and popcorn for a little while. Now hold on tight because we've got to get past a few camera lenses."

She muttered a couple curse words under her breath, a testament to how nervous the press attention made her. Determined to get her past the reporter vultures who now knew where she spent her free time, Wes ushered her toward her building. They passed a homeless guy sleeping on a hunk of cardboard beneath an awning and a couple dressed in sweats walked their dogs in the unseasonably mild winter weather, carrying a steaming box of take-out pizza between them.

Darting around the press hounds and into the building with only a few flashbulbs blinding him in the process, Wes caught himself envisioning him and Tempest walking together like that. As if they belonged together.

His wrist itched where his tattoo rested, reminding him of the poison ivy effect of women in his life. A knee-jerk reaction after all these years, no doubt. Logically, he knew New York was filled with great women. It was finding the right one that seemed more daunting than tracking a killer.

Tempest wasn't the kind of woman he would have ever pictured himself with, but he had to admit, he'd never been with a woman who would give up roses because her dog had allergies. Maybe there was a chance...

Maybe he'd suddenly morph into a stand-up guy willing to put his neck in the noose for incredible sex and a few good laughs? Seemed bloody unlikely. Hell, he put himself on the line enough at work without dishing up his guts in his personal life, too.

"Is that how long you see us lasting?" Tempest smoothed the collar of the coat back into place once they were safely inside the building. "A little while?"

"You'd get sick of me if I stuck around any longer than that." His gaze scanned the flight of stairs and the rows of mailboxes just inside the front door. Except for an old Beatles tune drifting from one of the apartments downstairs, all was quiet tonight.

"Is that what your girlfriends say when they leave you? They're sick of you?" She started for the stairs but he drew her back, pointing to the elevator which seemed a safer route. Staircases were notorious locations for crime because they were usually more isolated. Did she usually take the stairs by herself?

"No. Usually they say something to the effect of, 'Hey, Wes, meet Jack, the new man in my life.'" He steered her into the ancient elevator car and pressed the button for the third floor. "But I tend to interpret that as being sick of me."

"Hmm." She fiddled with the lapel of her coat, making him recall exactly what she had on underneath.

Nothing.

"What do you mean, *hmm?* Don't go playing psychologist on me today." He pointed a finger in her smiling face. "My partner already took a turn and I think one amateur shrink a day is all I can handle."

"I just wondered if you chased away these women on purpose." Her dark eyes flicked over him with curious intent. "I can't picture anyone being dumb enough to play you for a fool."

The elevator chimed, saving him from having to tackle that one.

"You'd be surprised." He held the elevator door while she stepped out, already thinking how many ways he could distract her as soon as they made it to her door. His gaze zeroed in on the belt of the trench coat and he wondered how fast he could have her naked.

"Oh, my God." She stopped short in the hallway, the tremor in her voice snagging his attention faster than a felony in progress.

Reaching her side in two strides, he caught sight of what had her so upset. The door to her apartment had been spray painted with graffiti, spelling out in fire engine–red letters—*Home of Whores 'R' Us*.

Rage spilled over him, an emotion he'd seldom encountered in ten years of crime scenes far more gruesome than the vandalism on Tempest's door. But this was different. This had happened to *her.*

The Chelsea apartment was her home, the place she'd bought to give herself the sense of belonging her family never had. And some worthless jackass had mounted a campaign to steal that from her along with the work that was so important to her.

"I'll find whoever did this." Wes slid an arm around Tempest, yanking himself out of his own fierce thoughts long enough to reassure her. He lowered his voice, tucking her close as he scanned the third floor for any hint of movement. "The paint is still wet, so the perp might be close. Do you know anyone well enough in the building to stay with for a few minutes while I look around?"

"No." She shook her head with fast, jerky movements. "No one. And I need to check on Eloise."

Her skin had paled, her whispered words breathless with a hint of panic.

Damn. Investigative work would have to be put on hold.

"Wait here while I make sure the security system is still armed and then we'll check on her together."

He tested the lock and found it still engaged before obtaining the day's code from Tempest. She could reprogram later. Right now, he needed to make sure her apartment was safe.

Safe?

He knew damn well she wouldn't rest easy until he caught whoever threatened her. For that matter, he wouldn't rest easy, either.

Like it or not, Tempest was about to get the best alarm system on the market. Since her stalker could very well be a killer, Wes would make sure she received around-the-clock watch from New York's finest.

Him.

TEMPEST WATCHED Wes shake hands with a couple of his cop friends two hours later and knew for a fact she'd never be able to get a good night's sleep in her apartment again. She didn't care that Wes had just sworn up and down her home hadn't been broken into this time, she still felt violated. Watched. Vulnerable.

He'd put in a call to his precinct and wrangled some help lifting prints from her door and an empty can of spray paint found in her hallway, but he wasn't optimistic they'd get anything. Mostly, he'd said it was important to keep a paper trail of the criminal activity so that when he caught the perpetrator, they'd have the right ammunition to prosecute under the harsher stalker laws.

Which was all fine and good, but it didn't give her any assurance she'd be able to sleep here tonight. Or any night for that matter. No matter how many kick-boxing classes she attended, she'd never feel strong enough to fight off someone filled with so much hate. Shivering, she tucked her feet between the couch cushions and snuggled closer to Eloise, who she allowed on the furniture only for special occasions.

Like when she was scared spitless.

She'd traded in Wes's trench coat for a pair of sweats and a long sleeved T-shirt that said "Sculptors Do It With Their Hands," a giveaway from an art workshop she'd attended during college. Somehow the "Whores 'R' Us" on her doorway had made her want to cover up, sending her running for comfort clothes even though Wes and his cop friends had covered the offending message with black plastic until she could paint over it.

"Are you okay?" Wes's gray eyes were dark with concern as he headed toward her place on the couch after locking her front door behind his friends.

"I'll be better once you find out who hates me so damn much." She gave Eloise a final squeeze before nudging her off the couch. Time to be a grown-up and figure out what to do next. "I definitely don't want to cross paths with this person face-to-face."

"You need better protection." He dropped down onto the couch beside her.

"I'm not going back to the Park Avenue house." She didn't realize how adamantly she opposed the idea until the protest spilled from her lips. But the home reminded her of all the reasons she'd never fit into her family, and all the ways she wanted to find her own path in the world. As soon as she hired a new CEO for Boucher, she was leaving her parents' superficial lifestyle far behind her so she could challenge herself. She'd been so wrapped up in wealth and privilege her whole life, she'd never had a chance to test her mettle. To see what she was made of.

"That's not what I had in mind." He'd dispensed with his jacket long ago and now sprawled on her sofa in his white shirt, the skinny purple tie loosened around his neck.

"I know the security is good there," she continued, still locked in her own thoughts. "But I'll never feel independent until I— What did you say?"

He picked at the elastic band around her ankle where her gray sweats met her bare skin. "I'm suggesting you bump up security here."

"But I just dumped half my month's salary into a system that—" She was missing something. His intent gray gaze told her as much.

"I'm going to be your new protection." He smoothed his hand up her calf where she'd folded her legs under her, then palmed her knee. "Say hello to your new bodyguard."

She hadn't realized she was already shaking her head until Wes frowned.

"What do you mean, *no?* I'm not giving you an option on this one." He tugged her leg closer, pressing her shin to his chest. "You need me here."

"I'll figure out something." Letting Wes help her out now would be like opening the door to her heart with both hands and saying, *"Come on in! Do your worst."*

She couldn't allow herself to think about him as her protector or she'd never extricate herself from that safe, comfortable place until Wes left her high and dry and even more of a pampered, over-protected society princess than she'd always been.

"There's nothing to figure out." He sounded damn sure of himself for a man who wasn't in charge of her life. "I need to guarantee your safety, and I can't do that unless I'm with you 24/7."

"My safety is my own responsibility." Maybe she could hide out at a hotel for a few days. Although, if someone was watching her, it wouldn't matter where she went.

"Catching a killer is *mine*. And if that means I have to camp out here until this offender surfaces again, then I'm damn well going to do it."

"I'm never here when your suspect arrives. If you're watching me all the time, you won't even be here when the guilty party shows up because you'll be too busy following me to snooze-fest board meetings and running from camera-happy journalists."

Shrugging, he didn't seem too concerned. "I'll have Vanessa watch the apartment while we're out."

She should be grateful the New York Police Department would go out of its way to offer her around-the-clock watch, but instead, she found herself wondering how many other at-risk women in NYC received this kind of five-star treatment.

Tempest the Over-Privileged Strikes Again.

She could already see the headlines.

Knowing she couldn't argue her way around him, however, she simply nodded, committing herself to his plan until she could come up with a better answer. Yet even as she gave him permission to insinuate himself deeper into her life and her heart, Tempest found herself wondering how she'd ever forge the independence she sought.

11

WES COULDN'T REMEMBER the last time he'd caught a lucky break, so his minor victory with Tempest— even if her agreement was grudging at best—definitely tasted sweet.

He skimmed a hand up her sweats-clad thigh, knowing it would probably take more finesse than he possessed to get her naked again tonight. "You won't even know I'm here."

"In a studio apartment?" She lifted a delicately arched brow, her honey eyes glowing with a fire he guessed had more to do with frustration than desire.

Still, a guy could always hope.

"I won't even bring Kong over to join the sleepover." He figured she deserved a few concessions after she'd given in without a marathon protest. "But we'll have to stop by my apartment now and then to make sure she has everything she needs."

"Kong, I could handle. No offense, Wes, and I'm grateful for the extra protection, but I've been trying to snag a little more independence this year and with you here…" She pulled the cuff of her shirtsleeve over one hand and twisted the end like a bread tie as if to cover as much of herself as possible.

As if she could retreat inside her clothes.

Wes wondered if that trick had worked for her in the past and why she liked to hide from a life most people would have considered a dream come true.

He fished inside her sleeve and tugged her hand free before raising it to his lips. "This doesn't have to be a prison sentence for you. I can go with you to work, or wherever you need to be."

Although, now that he thought about it, the arrangement would make it tough to track suspects when he was committed to be at Tempest's side all day. Then he had a whole host of dates lined up for tomorrow, too. Damned if he knew how to handle winnowing through the next round of possible suspects with Tempest by his side. He'd hardly look like a bachelor with her there.

"I can take off a few days." She brushed a dark curl out of her eyes, a silver bangle glinting at her wrist and making an incongruous touch with her sweats. "I'm sure you've got work of your own and I can devote some time to my sculpting. I'll never have a gallery showing if I don't start replacing the broken pieces."

"You're probably safest in the apartment anyhow now that you've got the security system." Maybe he could have Vanessa stay with Tempest for a few hours tomorrow while he followed through on his dates. "I think that's why your stalker had to be content with spray painting the door this time. I don't think our vandal could penetrate the security."

"I'll call my office and let them know I won't be there in the morning." She picked up the phone from its cradle beside the couch while Wes ran through the new evidence in his head.

When Tempest's apartment had first been trashed, he'd thought the perpetrator might be a pro based on the clean pick of the lock on the front door, even though the rampant destruction within had seemed like a very personal statement. But the spray-painted message tonight confirmed her intruder wasn't a professional criminal. The "Whores 'R' Us" label on her front door had been an emotional act, a crime of anger and passion.

He watched Tempest hang up the phone, wondering where to start with his new line of questioning. She seemed reluctant to venture near her past, but he couldn't avoid it anymore.

"What's your take on the note your detractor left on the door?" On a personal level, he didn't really want to know about past lovers and old boyfriends, but as a cop, he needed to uncover the truth. "Do you have anyone in your life who's said things like that to you before?"

His first instinct on the murder case told him the killer had been a woman since his victim was still naked when they found him, his autopsy confirming he'd been engaged in sexual relations within an hour of the time of death. A woman's negligee had been found at the crime scene, but they'd had no luck tracing the garment to any "blonde from MatingGame" as referenced in the victim's appointment book.

Between that evidence and the fact that the victim had penciled in an appointment with someone from MatingGame on the night of his death, Wes had focused on female suspects, even running a check on the old lady who lived a few doors down from Tempest.

But the message on Tempest's door tonight made him second-guess his conclusions. Why would a hooker leave a message about Whores 'R' Us? Wouldn't a prostitute be more defensive of her profession?

Unless the suspect wanted to draw negative press down on Tempest's head. In which case, the message emblazoned in red all over the front door had been a cagey move.

Shaking her head, Tempest unfolded her legs from underneath her and settled back on the sofa. "Never. I told you, I don't date much because it gets too complicated. The last guy I saw a movie with ended up in the newspapers, and so did you."

He waited, hoping his patience would allow her to think through the people in her life and come up with a more solid lead because right now, he didn't have much.

Shrugging, she splayed open palms skyward as if to suggest she had no idea. "I just assumed the message must relate to MatingGame and your suspicion that it's connected to prostitution."

A likely guess. And yet...

"Not many people know about MatingGame's possible darker side," he reminded her. "It's still one of the most popular singles spots on the Internet."

"So you don't think the average person would trace a connection between me and an escort service." She shifted on the couch so she could turn and face him. "Makes sense. So either Whores 'R' Us is a reference made by someone in the know, or else…"

She stopped short before her gaze narrowed as she looked up at him. "You think the words were intended as a personal slam? On *me?*"

He didn't need a psych degree to know he'd offended her. She bristled and huffed, straightening in her seat.

"In my business, it pays to check out every angle. And I still think our offender might be a woman, but in light of the message left for you tonight, it can't hurt to consider male suspects as well. Some guys will dole out some pretty harsh treatment once they get their asses dumped. That's no reflection on you or any woman who ends up with a psycho bastard on her tail."

"You're right." She slumped back next to him, her movement stirring the scent of her almond fragrance. "I'm just a little touchy on the dating subject."

"Touchy? Talk to me, Tempest." He stroked a hand over her cheek, his mind turning over possible scenarios for what happened here tonight. "I can't think through this unless you shed a little more light on your past or any men who might have it in for you."

"Honestly, there's almost nothing to share because my parents always gave me a hard time no matter who I dated. Guys in their social circle were written off as complacent trust-fund babies who would never go anywhere on their own. Guys who came from more diverse backgrounds were seen as too uncultured to squire me around to family business commitments. I always found it easier to just avoid romance all together, and I don't think any guy ever got close enough to me to be mad I didn't pay more attention to him."

"Then I'm going to keep looking into female users of the Blind Date service in case a woman has been behind the break-in and the vandalism tonight, but I'm also going to broaden my search because something's not sitting well with me about that theory." His thoughts shifted, trying to put a male suspect into the killer's shoes.

When she seemed lost in thought, he set aside his continual mental review of the crime. They'd been so close to jumping into bed together tonight—until they'd come home to find the painted message on her front door. He told himself a gentleman would hold back, but that didn't stop him from wanting her.

Remembering about Tempest's lack of dating history, he wondered if her mother had eased up on her since her father had died. He sure as hell hoped so, because Tempest deserved to be loved. "You know, maybe for your mom and dad, it was just a classic case of no one being good enough for their daughter. I'll bet there are lots of great parents who think the same thing about their kids."

He eyed her as she twirled her silver bangle on her wrist, thinking he'd rather be stripping off that and a whole lot more. Too bad his attempts to charm her—or even just put her at ease—were falling flat in a hurry.

"That's a nice thought, but I don't think it fits my folks." Rolling the bracelet between her palms, she peered up at him through long, dark lashes. "Did I tell you I already received the call from my mom about you?"

"She saw an imposter on the social pages, I take it?"

"She's been living in London for three years now, but she still subscribes to three New York daily papers. My phone was ringing by noon so she could give me an earful."

"I'll bet it was nothing compared to the crap I took at work." Refusing to concern himself with Tempest's mother's opinion, he thought maybe he'd be better off redirecting. "Aside from a few not-so-subtle hints that any picture in the paper where I wasn't kicking ass made me a pretty boy, I also got serenaded by two guys playing Puccini on harmonica since a social page photo must mean I dig opera."

A giggle snuck free from her somber mood, giving him hope he could still get her to talk. And encouraged him maybe later they could *not* talk for a few hours and communicate on a level where he was a hell of a lot more fluent.

"Sorry about that."

"It's okay. There's a guy on the force who's married to a fashion critic, and he left me a sympathy card since he's been through it all with his high-profile wife." The hand-drawn comic of Wes in a hangman's noose had helped him shake off his frustrations today. Especially since it came from Josh Winger, who along with his partner Duke Rawlins, posted one of the highest arrest rates in the precinct.

When silence met his words, Wes realized the word "wife" still echoed ominously through the room.

And even though there wasn't any chance he'd work things out long-term with Tempest, Wes couldn't help but wonder how a regular guy like Josh had married into glitz and fame while still keeping plenty of street cred on the force.

It had taken Wes a year and a half just to recommit himself to being a cop after Steve's death. And now that he had, he wouldn't allow any uncomfortable conversations to keep him from getting the answers he needed.

Changing the topic abruptly, he called on the blunt approach that always seemed to work when finesse failed.

"So you're sure that no one you've dated could be behind the spray-paint job. What about guys you've turned down? Maybe somebody is upset you said no?"

She thought for a minute before shaking her head—her dark, silky hair an enticement his fingers could scarcely resist. "I've been pretty secluded ever since my dad died, so there haven't been that many people who've gotten close enough to ask me out. My life has been all about work up until January, when I decided to take the studio apartment and make some changes."

From Wes's perspective, it had been about damn time since her parents obviously did a number on her just because she hadn't wanted to follow in their footsteps.

"Then maybe we ought to focus more on your workplace. Tell me about this Katrina— No, wait. You called her Kelly? Tell me more about her."

TEMPEST DIDN'T WANT to think someone she worked with could be so vindictive. Had Kelly really resented Tempest bringing MatingGame on board enough to write something as foul as *Whores 'R' Us* on her front door?

But still, she appreciated Wes's need to cover all his bases. Besides, the sooner he solved his case, the sooner he'd be out of her life and she would be free to salvage some of her fractured independence. As much as the idea of being alone again stung, she knew it only made sense to talk to him.

"She's been with the company for eight years." Tempest dug out everything she knew about Kelly, including the fact that she'd been relentlessly vying for the CEO spot and that she'd never brought a date to a single corporate function.

Maybe it didn't matter—and Tempest certainly preferred to attend professional parties stag, too— but at this point, she figured she might as well spill everything she could think of about Kelly, Boucher Enterprises and her work there.

Two hours later, she had to admit Wes was a great listener. Or was he just a great cop? Tired and confused, she couldn't be sure if it had been the man or the detective who listened to her, but she knew she wouldn't last an hour more before sleep overtook her.

"You okay?" Wes tucked a finger under her chin and tipped her face up to gaze into her eyes. "You look beat."

"Gee, thanks." She slumped deeper into the couch, heart sore at the way her night had rapidly disintegrated ever since they got back to her place. Thank God Wes had been with her. "I'm just trying to process so much ugliness in the world. I'm depressed after having my apartment ransacked and then vandalized, but you must see so much worse than that every day. Doesn't it bring you down?"

"Not usually. Most of the time it fires me up to fix things. I catch the bad guys, and all is right with the world again." He switched gears faster than her high-tech ten-speed bicycle, obviously not prepared to dwell on his work. "Sorry for asking you to take the stroll down memory lane tonight, but maybe something you told me will help the pieces fall into place."

"I hope my boring life didn't put you to sleep." Relating all the stories about Boucher made her realize how little she'd ventured outside her safety zone despite her New Year's resolution to be her own person.

She had an apartment and a passion for sculpture and soaps. But how often did she get out in the world to meet new people and see new things? Knowing Wes had made her want to be more adventurous. To take a few chances.

"Nope." He shifted on the couch, slinging his arm along the back of the sofa to dangle one hand just above her shoulder. "But it did make me wonder how you could stand the isolation with no dates and no…"

When his words trailed off, she caught the heat in his gaze, the subtle arch of a questioning brow.

"You mean no sex?" It had been a long time for her before her conference table interlude with Wes. A very long time.

Since she had the feeling Wes was Mr. Sexual Experience, she had no intention of admitting he was only her second sex partner.

"Not sex *per se,* but the pleasure of physical contact. The kisses. The touching." He shook his head all of a sudden. "And it's not a damn bit of my business."

She had the feeling he was just playing the gentleman for her tonight after the ugly message on her front door, but something told her Wes still wanted her the same way she still wanted him. The angry words her stalker had left hadn't erased the hunger she felt for Wes. If anything, she only craved the sensual connection with him all the more.

"Who says I went without touches?" She decided it couldn't hurt to have a little fun with Wes tonight and up the heat with some suggestive conversation.

And maybe she was a smidge offended that he looked at her years of abstinence with what seemed damn close to pity, when that time had helped her to look past sex and desire to see what people really wanted from her.

Of course, that trick hadn't worked with Wes. She still had no idea what he wanted from her since desire had clouded her well-trained eyes from the moment he first strolled into her apartment.

"I got the impression you closed the door on men for a few years." He straightened, his posture no longer lazy and comfortable, but tense and alert.

The new topic of conversation seemed to have his full attention. And didn't that soothe her old insecurities? She couldn't help but enjoy the way Wes took a definite interest in her and her sexual experiences.

"Don't discount the value of solo pleasure." Her heart beat faster at the frank interest in Wes's smoky gray gaze. "I assure you, I can bring myself to orgasm faster than any man on the planet."

Understanding lit his gaze as he followed her line of thinking.

"You realize you've just issued a challenge I can't refuse?" Mischief danced in his dark eyes as he leaned closer.

"That's not a challenge, it's a fact. I'm living this body from the inside, Detective, so it only makes sense that I know exactly what revs it up." What was it about the male psyche that fueled men to tout their sexual prowess at every given opportunity? "It's a physiological advantage no man could fully compete with, although I'll be the first to admit I'd rather have your hands on me than mine."

She scooted closer to him on the couch, putting herself in easy reach. She didn't think she'd recover this level of desire after coming home to find her apartment vandalized. But maybe she needed to be with Wes tonight to feel whole again. Strong. The fears and the worries of a few hours ago faded away as the temperature soared between them.

"You'd prefer I touch you, yet you think you can make yourself hit your personal high note faster than me?" He grinned wickedly, but didn't venture any closer to her.

"It's just biology." And very unimportant considering the way her heart slugged harder against her ribs. She'd had enough time in her life to experience the limited joys of solo sex. As long as Wes was within reach, she planned to make decadent use of that lean, strong body of his. "Besides, the orgasms are much better when there is a friend to share them with."

Refusing to wait for him to touch her any longer, she picked up his hand and tucked it under her shirt. Farther, higher, until he covered her lace-trimmed breast with his palm.

"Really?" Flexing his fingers, he squeezed gently. "What if you did the stroking, but a friend was around to watch? What caliber of orgasms would you achieve then, I wonder?"

Sidling closer, she arched more heavily into his hand, craving the heat of those strong, nimble fingers. She couldn't imagine playing out the scenario he suggested. The vision of him watching while she…

No doubt, it would be hot.

"I already flashed you in the alley." She moaned with pleasure as his other hand snaked up her shirt and molded around her other breast. "Don't you think I've been adventurous enough for one night?"

"Not even close. Whether you admit it or not, I'm guessing you've got a few years of abstinence to make up for. And lucky for you, I'm very glad to oblige." He tugged off her sweatshirt but left her bra on, his gaze lingering in a way that was oh-so-flattering.

"I *do* like it when you watch me," she admitted, wondering if those silver-gray eyes of his could turn any darker. They already glowed with steely intensity as he watched her slip off her sweatpants. She left her white lace panties around her hips since he seemed to like the visual of her lingerie and Tempest planned to give him an eyeful.

"I promise I won't even blink." True to his word, his gaze locked on her undergarments that were semitransparent. "Just tell me where you want me."

Glad he gave her full run of the show, she shouted an order to Eloise to stay put while she stretched out on the couch. She usually slept with the bed pulled out, but with her blood rushing through her veins in a geyser-hot flood, she didn't want to take the time to rearrange the furniture.

She wanted Wes's undivided attention. When he slid deep inside her tonight, she wanted to be able to look in his eyes. And when he found his release, she wanted to see that clench of his muscles, the sheen of sweat over his velvety skin.

Wes made her feel too beautiful, too sexy, to hide behind a silken blindfold.

"You can sit right there." She left him on the edge of the couch while she flung one leg over his lap, the other resting on the cushions behind him.

Leaning back on a mountain of throw pillows, she peered down the length of her smooth pale skin to his muscular thighs, lean waist and square shoulders. He'd stripped off his shirt and tie at some point, his trousers only partially zipped but still clinging to his hips. His erection strained the fabric even with the fly loosened, his white cotton boxers stretching over the bulge that reached above the waist.

Come to mama.

Breath catching in her throat at the sight of all that delectable manhood on display, she decided she'd never had better inspiration for skimming her fingers over her panties. Simply put, he was the most fascinating man she'd ever met.

Goose bumps broke out over her skin as he followed the progress of her fingers with his gaze. The silk and lace of her lingerie grew damp with heat, the fabric molding intimately to her as she traced a circle around the hard knot of her clit.

Her hips twitched at the thought of him touching her, and with his big male body positioned between her legs, it was easy enough to imagine his hands on her, too. She tugged aside the lace to stroke the slick folds beneath. Little spasms fanned out from her womb, warning her it wouldn't be long until the bigger contractions came, the ones that would wring her body from the inside out.

All because he was here. Watching. Devouring her with his gaze.

Her fingers tracked faster over her flesh grown swollen with want, her fantasies turning more graphic as she imagined him bending over her, taking her in his mouth. Lapping at her most sensitive places.

And then it was no dream.

With a growl of pure animal hunger, he leaned over her, tugging her panties down and off with one hand while he guided her fingers to his mouth with the other. One by one he sucked each digit in turn, tasting her with a thoroughness that left her whole body humming for that most intimate of kisses.

Hot breath fanned over her, stoking the fiery tension inside her. Tighter. Higher.

When he swirled his tongue over her sex she flew apart on contact, her screams thankfully muffled behind Wes's accommodating hand. Lush spasms rolled over and over her, rocking her insides with raw sexual heat until she shuddered from the force of them.

Only then did he pull her up off the couch and into his lap to straddle him, lowering her down onto his shaft. He'd managed to put a condom on, but his pants were still at half-mast, the zipper threatening her most sensitive places until she shoved the trousers down with a trembling hand.

And then she thought no more, surrendering herself completely to the fierce rhythm he set. Her fingers gripped his shoulders as she anchored herself against the next round of waves already dragging her under. Deeper.

Gasping in one last breath, she let her release overtake her as another climax swept through her damp body. Wes didn't bother quieting her cries this time, his own echoing moments behind hers. Their heartbeats hammered so close together the rhythms became indistinguishable, their timing as in synch now as it had been while they made love.

Or had sex.

Or whatever it was they'd just done.

Tempest had no idea. She could barely think. Couldn't move. Couldn't believe she'd just touched herself for the sensual delight of a man she'd known for all of—how long had it been?— five days.

But, oh God, had it been good.

Body brimming with happy endorphins, she tried not to worry about what it meant that she'd just shared the best sex of her life with a man who'd made it very clear he wasn't a relationship kind of guy. If only she could look at sex like a man, taking her pleasure where she could and to hell with the consequences.

But as Wes guided them down to recline on the couch, his strong arms cradling her close to his heart, Tempest knew she'd crossed some kind of personal line with him tonight. She'd given him too much of herself, shared a little piece of her soul when she'd only meant to follow an intense attraction until it flared out of its own accord.

Too bad she hadn't fully comprehended what it meant to play with fire.

As she drifted off to sleep beside him, wrapped in the musky male scent of him, she told herself she'd figure out some solution in the morning. There had to be a way to reclaim her independence before she fell head over heels for a man who pushed her boundaries as no one else had ever done.

Somehow, she needed to put some space between them again before her old insecurities chased Wes away for good. Until she was strong enough to be a real partner for Wes, she'd keep her distance to make sure neither of them got burned beyond repair.

12

"OUCH!"

Wes suppressed the string of curses that swelled in his throat the next morning as he nicked his jaw with the plastic straight razor he'd unearthed from a new bag in Tempest's medicine cabinet. Why was it that a microscopic cut from shaving stung ten times more than a gushing flesh wound?

One of those mysteries of life. Kind of as pointless as trying to figure out why walking away from Tempest would hurt exponentially more than the hits to his ego from women who'd taken him deep in the past.

Setting aside the instrument of terror that had left three fresh cuts on his mug, Wes rinsed his face and dried off. Steam from his shower still hung thick in the black-and-white, art deco bathroom as he swiped the towel across the wrought-iron mirror in an effort to clean up after himself.

The shower and shave had done little to clear his head. Sleeping with Tempest again only made him want more, inciting primitive urges to hold her by his side that same way night after night. Maybe part of him had hoped the heat between them would cool after they'd been together a few times, but that was far from the case. If anything, he only wanted her now more than ever.

Flinging a towel over his shoulder, he slid into his clothes, wondering if she'd be awake yet. He'd forced himself to get up and shower instead of succumbing to the far more tempting pleasure of watching her sleep—her red, manicured fingers curled tightly around the sheet and tucked beneath her delicate jaw.

He was getting too close, too involved, the same way his old partner Steve had shortly before his death. Steve had fallen for one of the women involved in a crime ring he'd infiltrated. Wes had followed protocol and refrained from actively contacting his partner when he went silent three weeks into the job, but Steve had checked in with Wes on his own terms during the undercover stint, and his last message detailed his concern for getting his lady friend out safely. Wes still regretted respecting Steve's cover those last few weeks since the woman had ultimately exposed him.

Possibly turned him to crime, if the media coverage was to be believed.

Hanging the towel over the shower door, Wes reminded himself Tempest was nothing like that woman. For that matter, she wasn't anything like any woman he'd ever been with before, his type tending to stray more to fallen angels than uptown girls. What freaked him out was the loss of control when he started to care about somebody, the emotional sucker punch that reminded him it didn't matter how many arrests a guy made or street fights he'd won—when it came to women, men pretty much had no defense.

Except for the one-month rule, of course. Although it wasn't exactly ingenious, at least the time limit made sure he wouldn't be vulnerable to the relationship equivalent of a kick in the gonads.

Until now.

Apparently Tempest was like a fast-acting chemical agent to his system. A few rounds with her, and he was toast.

Frustrated and out of sorts, he yanked the bathroom door open, startling Eloise to jump up from her mat in the corner with a whine. Tempest lifted a curious brow from her spot in the kitchen where she swirled a tea bag around in a steaming ceramic mug, a morning rain shower beating hard at a window behind her.

"Ghost on your tail?" She shuffled toward a round table tucked in a corner of the studio near the oven range, a pair of ratty pink slippers scuffing along the dark hardwood floor. An untied terrycloth bathrobe flapped open over a T-shirt and a pair of blue plaid boxer shorts.

He refrained from mentioning the spook of morning-after doubts currently haunting her bathroom.

"Just in a hurry to see what New York's reigning society queen looks like in the morning." He wasn't ready to confront the questions between them. Not when he needed to step up his investigation today. Better to keep things light.

Dropping into a seat, she clutched her mug of tea

with both hands and smiled. "I'm presiding over an elegant table with perfect aplomb." She crossed her legs and kicked forward a slippered foot with a flourish. "And of course, I'm always a fashion plate. It just goes with the territory."

That's how she does it.

As Wes watched her bend over her tea and sip it with as much ritual and reverence as if it had been a life-saving elixir, he realized she was very good at making him feel comfortable with her wealth and privilege because she downplayed it at every turn. From her self-deprecating comments to her pared-down lifestyle, she gave off a common-person vibe that put him at ease.

But would she always be that way? Or would she tire of her Chelsea apartment and the struggling-artist scene once she'd gotten her fill of sculpting?

Not many people would be able to walk away from a world of luxury for long. Especially if they'd grown up accustomed to life's little extras the way she had.

Maybe he'd figure her out more now that he was staying with her for a few days. Get a better read on a woman who looked all wrong for him on paper, but in reality seemed very right.

"The slippers definitely make a statement." He wandered over to the stovetop and filled the empty mug she'd left waiting on the counter. Even in such a small thing, Tempest remained low pressure with her self-serve attitude.

Dropping the kettle back on a burner, he sifted through her basket of five thousand flavored teas looking for a bag that said plain old "Lipton."

"I don't think we should have sex anymore." Her pronouncement came just as he'd decided he'd try something called cinnamon zinger.

Damned if she hadn't zinged him first.

"Did I miss something here?" His tea bag floated on top of the water since he should have put it in the mug first. Assorted little details filled his cop brain, all the while refusing to process what she'd just said.

"I mean, I hope you'll still consider staying here until you catch the psycho-creep lurking around my apartment, but I don't think it's a good idea for us to keep up the intimacy."

She still clung to her teacup, only now Wes realized it wasn't just her magic elixir, it was a power potion that gave her the nerve to lob verbal bombs at him the morning after they'd shared something pretty damn profound.

"And you came to this conclusion while we were rolling off your couch for the third time last night? Or did you only just make up your mind this morning?" He sucked down his tea in one large gulp, the red-hot liquid frying the inside of his mouth. How in the hell could she be so casual?

"I'm sorry." Bowing her head for a moment, she seemed to study the wood grain in her floor before meeting his eyes again. "I didn't mean to be so abrupt, I just wanted to get the words out before I lost my nerve."

"At least you have the courtesy to admit it takes a hell of a lot of nerve to drop that on a guy at eight in the morning." His brain seemed as scalded as his throat since he couldn't figure out what else to say.

What *could* he say to that? "Care to tell me why you're changing your mind? Although, let's be very clear that this doesn't change a damn thing about me staying here. You're not getting rid of me until we catch whoever is stirring up trouble for you."

Nodding, she at least had the good grace to look relieved. Finally, she huffed out a sigh and looked at him dead-on.

"I'm a romantic." She said it with as much drama as if she confessed a cardinal sin.

"Considering my line of work, I'm usually pretty good at connecting the dots, but you're going to have to help me out on this one because I'm not following." He strangled the water out of his tea bag before flinging it in the trash.

And he thought he'd been confused about Tempest while he shaved this morning? He hadn't known the half of it.

Now there weren't just morning-after spooks on his tail. There was a whole legion of niggling regret demons and one very pissed-off ghost of what might have been.

SHE MIGHT HAVE PLANNED this better.

In the past eight months, she'd learned how to run a board meeting, mastered a travel schedule to oversee her offices abroad and played mediator to countless interdepartmental spats. Surely she could have devised a way to broach this subject with Wes in a way that didn't put him so far on the defensive he was seething at the other end of her kitchen, the steam rising off him faster than their freshly boiled tea.

Too bad she'd been afraid to go to sleep last night, terrified she'd wake up so out of her mind in love with the man in her bed that she would never be free of him. She hadn't even learned how to master her own insecurities. She was jealous that he met with strange women to crack a possible prostitution ring, for crying out loud.

Any guy noble enough to put his neck on the line as a cop didn't deserve that kind of anxiety from his partner. Girlfriend. Whatever she was supposed to be to this man who freely admitted he'd never been able to make a relationship work before.

If only he could give her some time to forge her own path first. To find her own strengths and get a handle on her own dreams. Maybe then she'd be able to commit herself to being the kind of woman Wes deserved. She just needed some more room to breathe. More space to think things through before they plowed ahead at breakneck speed.

"I thought I could brazen out an affair with you, Wes, but I can't. At least, not right now. I'm an old-school, hearts-and-flowers type of girl no matter how tough I try to be in the business world. And I just can't find it in myself to cut off my feelings from sex and simply enjoy what we have." At least, that was part of it.

They didn't need to delve into her lack of confidence now, did they? It was tough enough to deny herself the man she cared about without picking apart her psyche, too.

"Who the hell expects you to cut off your feelings from sex?" He gulped down another slurp of tea that had to singe all the way down. "I sure as hell have feelings about you, and I damn well expect you to have feelings about me after the conference room table, and the Park Avenue encounter, the alleyway…and that's not saying anything about last night."

"You have feelings for me?" Her feminine radar blinked wildly at the thought of this man harboring a hint of deeper emotions for her. All this time, she'd thought she was the only one whose heart was getting involved in their affair. "What kind?"

His brow furrowed as if she'd just asked him to solve quadratic equations. "Hell, I don't know. But you can bet I feel something when I'm with you."

Disappointment fizzled through her, renewing her decision to untangle herself from him before she had more to lose than great sex.

"Well if you ever figure it out, you be sure to let me know. I think we could both use a little time and space to find our footing with whatever is happening between us." She stared at the man she'd clung to half the night, feeding a frenzy of need inside her she hadn't even known existed. It wouldn't be easy to walk away from that, even knowing it was the right thing to do. "More tea?"

Dark clouds rolled through those gray eyes of his, warning her of the storm coming. She braced herself for a tirade in Wes's plainspoken style, but instead of arguing, he suddenly lifted his fingers to his lips and motioned for her to be quiet.

"What?" She peered around her studio, finally noticing Eloise standing on guard at the front door, her ears perking straight up as she stared at the knob expectantly.

Someone was outside her apartment.

Tension crackled as she watched Wes move stealthily across her floor, his steps soundless despite his long strides. For a moment, she hoped maybe it was the paperboy, and then she remembered she didn't subscribe to a paper.

And anyone who wanted to see her should have buzzed in downstairs.

Maybe it could be a neighbor loitering around the hall, looking for a lost key? The superintendent changing a lightbulb? Her brain rushed to supply scenarios even as her gut instinct gave her a bad feeling. She swallowed back a wave of fear, knowing Wes could handle whatever came his way. Still, what if her would-be intruder had a gun? Or worse, what if more than one person lurked outside her door?

She rose, unable to sit still while Wes confronted her problems by himself. She might not be a trained professional, but she had a vested interest in seeing her antagonizer brought low.

Her bravado held right until Wes's gun flashed, the dull gleam of silver sending a chill through her. She paused a few feet behind Eloise while Wes positioned himself by the door and motioned for her to get back.

Too bad her ancient fuzzy slippers were rooted to the floor beneath her. She bent down near Eloise, ready to vault into action if anyone bothered her dog, guns be damned.

Wes reached for the door handle, utterly silent as he listened. Waited. Jerked the door open with a start.

His gun glinted in front of a woman's face.

Kelly Kline's face.

Her hands whipped over her head, raised in surrender, skin going pale on the other side of Wes's gun.

"I'm just here to see Tempest."

Scrambling to her feet, Tempest walked closer to the standoff where Wes drew her co-worker inside, never taking his gun off her.

"It's okay, Wes. She works with me."

He snorted. "All the more reason to suspect her."

Kelly's eyes widened. "You're the guy from last night." She looked from Wes to Tempest, her gaze lingering on her CEO. "Is he here against your will?"

"He's a detective," Tempest inserted, thinking to put her at ease, even though now she was starting to wonder if Kelly's visit today had been a social one.

Could her ambitious VP be vindictive enough to go after Tempest if her path up the career ladder had been thwarted?

Wes pushed Kelly into a chair near the door while Eloise barked intermittently.

"I'll be asking the questions here. Just be kind enough to keep your hands where I can see them, Ms. Kline, and we won't have any problems." Wes tucked his weapon in the back of his trousers and kept his focus on Kelly. "Care to explain how you got into the building without Tempest buzzing you in?"

"A man coming out held the door for me." She crossed long legs in a pencil-slim skirt that rested just above her knees. "Since it was raining, I didn't think twice about coming inside and looking up Tempest on the directory. Now would you please tell me what this is about?"

Perhaps seeing the futility of firing questions at Wes, she directed a haughty stare toward Tempest.

Certain Wes wanted to run the show with their visitor, she said nothing.

"Not until you explain your reason for showing up here unannounced." The scowl on Wes's face suggested he didn't appreciate high-handed attitudes.

Tempest held her breath, wondering if Kelly would turn out to be the intruder who insisted she was in the wrong business. The Whores 'R' Us business.

"When I found out Tempest wouldn't be in the office today, I decided to track her down at home because what I have to say won't wait." Kelly smoothed her hands over her skirt before she looked Tempest in the eye. "I'm handing in my resignation."

"You're quitting?" She hadn't been prepared for that, considering Kelly had done everything but stand on her head to prove how committed she was to Boucher Enterprises. "You had so many plans for development, so many projects in the works overseas."

"Wait a minute." Wes reached out toward Kelly. "I'd like to see the letter please."

"That's between me and Tempest." Her coral-painted lips curled. "And you haven't even explained to me what's going on here. If I'm going to be greeted by a gun in the face, I think I've earned the right to know why."

"The NYPD is helping Ms. Boucher find out who's been harassing her. And you're welcome to leave if you can produce the letter of resignation you say you were submitting today."

"Well I can't do that because I haven't actually drawn it up yet. I wanted to speak to Tempest about what terms I might expect."

As if. The woman was insane if she thought she could dictate terms for quitting.

Wes didn't look overly impressed with her answer either. Nor did he seem any more pleased with the hedging answers she went on to give about her whereabouts the night before, after she'd left Mick's Grill, or her reasons for using MatingGame's services in the first place.

She maintained her dating life was her personal affair, and that she'd gone straight home after meeting Wes. A fact which no one could vouch for since she lived alone and hadn't seen anyone on her way into her apartment.

After another half hour of circular conversation and petulant answers, Wes allowed Kelly to leave with a reminder that she needed to conduct all business with Tempest at the company headquarters and not a private residence.

When the apartment door finally slammed shut behind her co-worker, Tempest didn't even know where to begin. She had more reason than ever to suspect Kelly was up to no good, although Wes said it would be difficult to prove anything until she made her next move.

Did that mean Tempest needed to wait for an escalation in violence against her?

And as if that weren't unsettling enough, she also hadn't even succeeded in getting Wes to agree their affair was over. But with a whole new set of fears and worries churning through her, she didn't know if she could find the emotional fortitude to debate the merits of a relationship built on lust today.

Now, she watched Wes as he stared out the window toward the street, thudding his forehead lightly on the glass. Making sure Kelly really left?

He turned toward her after a long moment, swiping a hand through his dark hair.

"She's lying about why she came over here." He stalked restlessly around the apartment, his body tense as if every muscle was coiled with tension.

Tempest said nothing, sensing he'd entered some kind of thinking zone and hadn't really been talking to her anyhow.

He paced a few more steps and stopped. "And we know she uses MatingGame to meet men. But is she strong enough to—" Pivoting on his heel, he focused on her. "Do you know if she works out?"

Confused, she shook her head. She'd only been on board with the company for eight months, and Kelly had probably been out of the country half that time.

"The murder victim was strangled," Wes continued, picking up his pace again until Eloise barked at him, tail wagging. "And whoever did it would have needed a hell of a lot of muscle."

Tempest bent to quiet her dog while that bit of information rolled over her. Strangulation? Somehow it seemed more brutally cold than a gunshot. She wondered why she hadn't asked Wes about it before.

Her fingers went to her throat, seeking the reassurance of her favorite quartz pendant until she remembered she hadn't worn it today. She was still loafing around the apartment in her bathrobe.

Before she could ask Wes more about how the murder case related to the break-in and vandalism at her apartment, the doorbell rang, raking along nerves already worn raw. This time at least, her visitor had used the buzz-in system connected to the downstairs door.

"That'll be my partner," Wes supplied as he moved toward the intercom speaker and exchanged a few words with a woman on the other end. Turning back to Tempest, he pushed the buzzer to admit the newcomer. "I called her before I took a shower this morning so she could swing by for a couple of hours."

Wes worked with a woman?

A stupid concern when ten thousand other worries bombarded her from all sides, but Tempest couldn't deny the flash of jealousy at the thought.

"You asked your partner to come here?" Why hadn't she at least taken a shower this morning? She probably looked like she'd been cut from one of those real-life cop shows where the women were always wearing mangy bathrobes with their hair shooting out of their heads in twenty different directions.

But logically, she knew that if she wanted Wes to solve his case, it would be a good thing for him to join forces with his partner instead of sacrificing himself to Tempest's insatiable new lust day after day.

"I've got to meet the next batch of women from Blind Date at Mick's this afternoon, but I trust Torres to keep you safe." Withdrawing his gun from the back of his pants, he flipped some little switch under the barrel before dropping it into a holster he'd slung over a chair.

Again with the dates?

She hated the idea of him spending all afternoon getting hit on by women from every borough in the city, but she held her tongue and slowly quelled her old insecurities, reminding herself that just yesterday she'd been looking for a way to get some distance between her and Wes. Today it seemed, she'd have it in spades.

There was a knock at the door behind her, startling her into realizing that Wes would be walking out to hunt for a killer who had strangled his last victim. And it dawned on her in that instant that her jealousy seemed petty and her need for distance seemed incredibly selfish. Right now, only one thing mattered.

She reached out to stop him before he could admit his partner, her hand clenching around his wrist.

"Be careful."

"You, too." Leaning in for a kiss, he covered her mouth with his and clamped his hand around her jaw, holding her steady while he tasted her one more time.

As he released her and Tempest stared up into his eyes, she already regretted that it would be their last.

13

WES WRENCHED OPEN Tempest's door, ready to lose himself in work since his personal life seemed to be disintegrating under his feet. Untangling a murder case seemed easy compared to comprehending the intricacies of the female mind. The taste of Tempest's kiss lingered on his lips as he spied his partner on the other side of the door.

Holding the leash of his 150-pound St. Bernard.

"You brought Kong?" His words were lost in an onslaught of barking and growling as the two dogs spied each other.

Eloise launched in front of Tempest to go head-to-head with the new canine in her territory. Vanessa's body lurched forward with the force of Kong's response, though she clung tenaciously to the leash.

"I thought it would be a nice surprise," Vanessa shouted over the din of woofing. "I didn't know she had a dog."

Tempest's voice cut through the noise. "Eloise, heel."

The terse words seemed to soothe the German shepherd, her barks quieting as she padded behind

Tempest, though her fur remained ruffled along the back of her neck.

Vanessa whistled appreciatively while she struggled with Kong. "That's an animal with some pretty manners."

Wes sighed as he took the leash from his partner. "Don't let her upstage my dog, Torres." Tugging harder, he shouted to Kong until he got her settled down and almost civil. "She's just a little more high-spirited."

Wes quieted Kong as he stroked her head, but there was nothing quiet inside him as he thought about walking out of Tempest's apartment. Sure it might be easier to leave now than to confront the whole host of concerns Tempest revealed this morning, but he'd been choosing that easy route for too long, continually opting for the path of least resistance when it came to relationships.

Something about Tempest made him want to work a little harder this time, to try his hand at untangling the knots and soothing the raw emotions exposed from their night together. And damned if the thought of losing her didn't make him reevaluate things. Rethink what he wanted out of his life.

After making introductions in the foyer, Wes watched the dogs circling each other and inspiration struck. A way to buy himself a little more time.

"Vanessa, how about you take Kong and Eloise down to the street and let them get more comfortable with each other on neutral terrain? They might relax faster that way and you can treat them to a snack." He hoped his partner would take the hint since he really needed a few more minutes with Tempest.

"Are you sure she can handle both of them?" Tempest bit her lip as she looked from the dogs to Vanessa and back. "They're pretty big."

"Vanessa's stronger than me. And she's a ninja." He dug in his wallet for a few bucks and jammed them in his partner's hand before she could protest. He clipped Eloise's leash to her collar and handed it to Vanessa. "She'll be fine."

He pried the door open behind her and steered her into the hallway as he lowered his voice for her ears alone. "I need five more minutes if I'm ever going to break the one-month barrier like we talked about. Got it?"

Understanding lit her eyes before Tempest followed them out.

"There's a pretzel vendor on the corner," Tempest called over his shoulder. "Eloise is usually more agreeable after a visit with him."

To Wes's relief, Vanessa nodded. Smiled. "No problem." She turned her gaze on him, however, and frowned. "And I'm *not* a ninja. I practice *kendo*, you damn cave dweller."

Steering the dogs toward the stairs, Vanessa walked away, lean muscles flexing as she wrangled the animals and began to lecture them about proper canine street etiquette.

Unwilling to waste his window of time with Tempest, he guided her back inside the apartment, closing the door behind them.

"What was that all about?" She eyed him warily,

her bathrobe swinging about her legs as she turned to face him. "What one-month barrier?"

Wes had forgotten women possessed bionic hearing.

"Inside joke." He held out the desk chair for her and waited for her to take a seat before he leaned on the desk. "Vanessa says I can't keep a relationship for more than a few weeks, hence the one-month obstacle. I hoped if she could give us a little more time together, I could figure out what happened to make you do the about-face this morning."

She frowned for a moment before her eyebrows lifted in tandem, her face the picture of surprise. "Because you want to break the one-month barrier with *me?*"

"You find that so difficult to believe?"

"A little." She reached for his hand, smoothing her thumb across the back of his knuckles and then up to the tattoo on his wrist. "You must know even better than me that it's tough to put yourself out there and trust in someone."

"Hell, yeah, I know. I'm a three-time loser in the trust department." He took her hand in his, halting her fingers in their quest. Vanessa told him he shouldn't always expect the worst from people, right? Maybe the time had come to charge into this mess with Tempest and expect—hope for—the best.

She opened her mouth to speak, but he had more to say on that subject. If he was going to put himself out there, he would do it all the way.

"Twice I lost out to women who would probably argue I chased them away by not being committed enough." Maybe they were right. But Wes had always felt like he gave it his best shot. "And a third time I trusted my partner could hold it together while undercover and was blown out of the water when he turned. I still can't fully believe he went rogue, but the reports from an investigation around his murder all point to him being waist-deep in criminal activity. You'd think I'd know better by now, wouldn't you?"

Tempest leaned forward in the desk chair, her hand brushing over his knee. "I'm sorry, Wes. I didn't know—"

"Doesn't matter." He interrupted the sympathetic words he didn't need anymore. He simply wanted another chance with her, and he was determined to secure it before he walked out of her apartment today. "What I'm trying to say is that maybe *I'm* the romantic and you're the cynic if I'm the only one willing to give this a chance."

It was the best he could do, the most forthright he could be. He'd put himself on the line for her this time, showing a side he hadn't shared with anyone for too many years. He didn't toss aside his pride and call himself a romantic for just anyone, damn it.

Tempest was special.

She blinked hard, as if trying to process what he was saying. Her brown eyes studied him intently.

"I'm not being cynical." She shook her head, denying the obvious. "It's called being practical. I've had my whole life on hold for the last eight months until I figure out who to entrust with my father's business. I'm caught between my dreams and my reality so often, I don't even know who I am half the time. That doesn't seem like a fair way to start a relationship."

"Who cares about fair? I'm not a demanding guy." He'd never asked much of any woman except fidelity for as long as they were together, and he knew without question that Tempest was the kind of woman who would view faithfulness the same way as him. Yet she wanted something else from him. Something he couldn't seem to understand. "You're busy and I appreciate that. So I'll take what you can give and we'll see how it goes."

"But *I* care about being fair," she said softly, seemingly unfazed by his appeal as she tied the belt on her bathrobe, cinching it closed. "And I'm not just worried about what's reasonable for you. When I'm ready to take the gamble with my heart, I want to give myself a real shot of making it work."

He didn't know how to argue his way around that without sounding like an insensitive jerk. His damn tattoo itched again, except he knew it wasn't the tattoo. It was just a stupid head-trip that surfaced with remarkable regularity whenever a woman talked about something like her heart.

"I'm not asking for forever, Tempest." He wasn't asking her to sign her name in blood, for crying out loud. He just wanted to be with her tomorrow. And the next day. And a few more afterward, if she'd let him.

"Believe me, I'm well aware of that." She managed a lopsided smile he'd never seen before, a grin that didn't look entirely happy to his eyes. "I just don't think we should jump into anything when you're not even sure what kind of feelings you have for me."

Hadn't he told her how he felt by asking her to stay with him and work things out? He'd given her more of himself than any other woman, and she was still turning him down. As the sound of dogs barking drifted up to Tempest's third-floor window, Wes realized his opportunity to convince her was over.

And he'd failed.

She wanted to know how he felt? He imagined his condition at this moment in time wasn't all that different from laying facedown on the street after fighting a losing battle. He'd been gutted and left to bleed out while her voice sounded farther and farther away.

The sensation gave him all the more reason to find Tempest's stalker today—to close his case and get on with life. Alone. No matter that he'd put himself on the line, risking heart and pride to a woman too caught up in her own life to make time for him.

There was nothing left for him here.

"WAS IT JUST ME, or did Wes seem a little out of it when he left?" Vanessa Torres had been low-key company for most of the afternoon, staying out of Tempest's way while she showered and then worked on a new sculpture, a male vampire figure with outstretched arms.

Tempest couldn't think of any other way to burn off the mixture of fear, frustration and regret suffocating her ever since Wes seemed to shut her out and had left the apartment without hearing her side of things.

But apparently Vanessa wasn't going to keep quiet on the subject of Wes all day.

"I just assumed he was getting himself into work mode." Tempest didn't want to discuss the trouble between her and Wes with a stranger, especially when she didn't even understand it herself. She only meant to ask him for more time to figure out what she wanted in life, a few more weeks to become the independent woman she knew she could be.

But somehow, Wes seemed to take that as a rejection, even going so far as to tune out half of what she said. Or so it seemed. She couldn't tell what happened any better than Vanessa, but she knew that—in Wes's eyes, at least—she had slighted him by not agreeing to forge ahead with a relationship even though she knew she wasn't ready.

"He's not usually like that at work," Vanessa observed lightly, watching Tempest mold the basic lines of the vampire's bare chest with her hands before she picked up a carving tool. "If anything, he's hyperfocused about the job and today he seemed a million miles away."

The comment echoed in the wide-open studio space, a weighted silence that seemed as much a presence in the room as the two dogs and two women.

She ignored it.

"Have you and Wes been working together for a long time?" Neatly changing the subject, she contemplated the shoulders of her vampire man and wondered what it would be like to be wrapped in those strong arms again.

Again?

Funny how Wes's image was all that came to mind for artistic inspiration today. She'd started work on her male creature to take her mind off Wes, and still found his face staring back at her from the dark, half-formed clay. Her heart ached with a wrenching sense of failure and loss ever since he'd walked out abruptly the moment Vanessa returned with the dogs.

Had she thwarted any chance of a future together by asking him to give her a little time?

"A year and a half." Vanessa stared out one of the windows at the misty rain that seemed to have enveloped the city for nearly a week, her sleek, dark hair falling in a smooth curtain over her profile. Tall and slim, she had the kind of posture Tempest's mother had failed to instill in her despite a considerable amount of effort. This woman possessed a natural poise and elegance that had always eluded Tempest. "He's one of the best detectives assigned to the precinct."

"He said his former partner died on the job." Tempest didn't mean to pry, but figured it couldn't hurt to open the doorway in case Vanessa cared to share anything that would help her understand Wes better.

Not that it mattered now, when she'd already told him she wasn't ready for a relationship. Regret pricked her, even as she knew her decision had been sound. Logical.

Painful.

"Wes *would* say that. He had a hard time believing Steve would do anything illegal." Vanessa traced a raindrop sliding down the glass with her fingernail. "But most people think his partner died after transforming himself into the alter ego he used for a cover. He wasn't as strong a cop as Wes—physically or mentally—and I think he suffered without his role model to keep him in line."

Tempest's fingers slid away from the wet clay, thinking how easily she could lose herself against the force of Wes's personality as well. It would be hard not to lean on someone who seemed so capable.

"Wes deserves a stronger partner." Tempest hoped Vanessa Torres provided that for him. The way Tempest figured, any woman who could single-handedly bring peace between Kong and Eloise possessed a fair amount of strength.

Vanessa peeled her attention away from the misty windowpane to meet Tempest's gaze with clear green eyes. "He sure does. Do you think you've got what it takes?"

Somehow Tempest wasn't surprised that Wes's partner would have a flair for direct speech. She shook her head, determined to be honest with Vanessa—and herself. "Not yet. But I'm working on it."

A ghost of a smile played over Vanessa's lips, but before Tempest could be certain it had been there, it was gone again, her face a smooth mask with wise eyes. "Let me know if there's any way I can help. Wes is a damn good guy—for a cop."

Tempest wondered briefly what Vanessa had

against the men on the force, but her most pressing concern now was how to make Wes understand all she wanted was a little more time.

Since he hadn't listened to her, maybe this time she needed to *show* him she was serious. They could have a shot at a future if only he'd give her some more time to pull her life together. To find her own strength.

"Actually, there *is* something you could do to help me." She hoped Vanessa would go for it, but there was a very real chance she might shoot down the idea without even hearing her out since it could be dangerous. "And at the same time, I'll be helping you sew up your investigation all the sooner."

SHE WOULD BE a strong partner, damn it.

Tempest clung to the thought like a personal mantra as she and Vanessa waited for Bliss Holloway, MatingGame's operations manager, to dispense with social niceties late that afternoon in the woman's midtown home.

Vanessa had quickly agreed they needed to hear from such a key figure in the investigation as soon as possible. Since Wes was in the middle of interviewing potential suspects, that meant Vanessa would talk to Bliss, even if it meant bringing Tempest along for the ride.

After days of silence following the break-in, the MatingGame manager had finally returned Tempest's phone call shortly after lunch. Vanessa and Tempest had set off together—an elegant street cop and a renegade socialite with little in common except for their united effort to help Wes close his files on the MatingGame killer.

The more Tempest thought about him interviewing suspects all afternoon, the more she worried. Maybe it was the way they'd parted that had unsettled her, but she couldn't shake a bad feeling about the day.

Now, she followed Bliss Holloway down a short corridor in a beautifully appointed suite where she said the three of them could talk privately. Bliss, a self-made millionaire before she was thirty, continued to conduct her business from the penthouse floor of an upscale hotel even though Tempest had offered to purchase corporate office space for MatingGame.

Bliss was a woman with unflagging energy and vision, the kind of lit-from-within personality that Tempest admired immediately. Her respect for the woman had only increased the longer they worked together since Bliss actively sought ways to donate portions of MatingGame's profit to private causes that helped a variety of underprivileged people from at-risk teens to low-income single mothers.

Her blond bob swung neatly across the shoulders of her jacket as she turned to look back at Tempest.

"I'll admit, I was worried when I got back from Tokyo this morning and heard your message." Their hostess led them into an open salon in the back of the penthouse after both Vanessa and Tempest had nixed her offer for tea. She gestured to a seating group near the fireplace and took a seat in an elegant wingback covered in dainty yellow flowers. "And now that you've arrived with a police detective in tow, I'm all the more concerned."

Briefly, Vanessa filled her in on the break-in and vandalism at Tempest's apartment, without mentioning the link to the murder they were investigating. And while Tempest had hoped Bliss would be able to offer an explanation that would somehow deflect attention away from the prostitution angle, instead she watched the woman's face turn pale.

"Someone wrote those words on your door?" Bliss turned to Tempest as if for confirmation, her fingers smoothing over a weighty tennis bracelet at her wrist. At Tempest's nod, she took in a deep breath. "What makes you think the vandals referred to MatingGame? Boucher Enterprises must own at least fifty companies worldwide."

Vanessa interrupted before Tempest could answer, no doubt wanting to be in control of an interview where crucial information could be at stake. "The police have additional evidence linking MatingGame to prostitution and perhaps to a more serious crime. Do you have any explanation for this, Ms. Holloway? Do you know of any women—or men, for that matter—using your dating service in an illegal manner?"

Bliss opened her mouth and closed it, as if unsure how to begin. When she tried again, her words were steady and calm. "To my knowledge, no one is using the service illegally, or I would have reported it immediately. But I'm afraid I may have information regarding the origins of the prostitution rumor."

Tempest sucked in a breath, nerves tense. If MatingGame turned out to be involved in something illegal, it could cost Boucher Enterprises millions in damage control and lost revenues. The hit to their credibility would trickle down through the company to hurt so many people, and yet Tempest couldn't stop herself from thinking she could withstand all of it if only the truth meant Wes wasn't in any danger tonight.

His safety meant more to her than anything.

"As MatingGame has become more commercially successful, I find myself with more opportunities than ever to reach out to people in the city who need a hand." She shifted in her wingback, adjusting her red-and-ivory-colored houndstooth skirt to cover her knees. "Recently, I needed some help around the office and because I work at home, I thought it would be okay to hire some young women away from their careers in the…um…*oldest profession* so they could have a fresh start."

Vanessa leaned forward in her chair, leather jacket squeaking. "You hired hookers?"

"I hired desperate women with small children who really needed a way out of their situations." Bliss straightened in her chair, spinning her words as smoothly as a trained politician.

"Where did you find call girls for hire, Ms. Holloway? I don't imagine you run into your average streetwalker on this block too often."

Bliss offered a tight smile, but her eyes remained cool. "This is New York, Detective. Let's not forget that no matter how lofty your address on Central Park West, you're still hovering on the edge of a playground for crime."

Tempest sensed a subtle tension between the women, but couldn't put her finger on it. Besides, right now, her sole concern was giving Wes whatever help she could to show him she was willing to work with him—for him—as soon as she got her own life straightened away.

She nudged into the conversation, hoping to speed things along. "So you met these women in the park?"

Bliss crossed her ankles beneath her chair. "No. I was simply making a point. I happen to have an old friend in the business who I've never managed to coax over to the other side, and I learned of these two troubled women from her."

While Vanessa continued to quiz the Mating-Game manager about the ex-hookers allegedly providing no more than clerical help, Tempest waited impatiently for their conversation to turn back to what seemed most important.

Finally, she interrupted them, too keyed up and worried about Wes to wait. "Do you have any reason to believe either of your office employees might be using MatingGame as a dating service?"

Bliss shook her head. "It's against the rules for direct company employees, and I post all of the MatingGame profiles so I would see any—" She halted abruptly, her fingers pausing in an idle dance across the tennis bracelet. "Unless they broke office policy and used Blind Date."

Perhaps she had the same bad feeling about the possibility as Tempest did, because Bliss was on her feet and hastening over to her computer before the words had all left her mouth. Vanessa and Tempest followed, their shoes sinking into the room's plush white carpet as Bliss's fingers flew across her keys.

"Should we call Wes?" Tempest whispered behind her hand while Bliss scanned page after page of data on a spreadsheet.

"We'll head over to Mick's Grill right after this and call him on the way." Vanessa never took her eyes off the computer screen.

Bliss paused her scrolling screen to point to an entry in the Web site user log. "This is it. Marianne Oakes's personal e-mail ID." She shook her head, eyes wide with disbelief. "I can't believe she would skirt the regulations and use our service after I gave her a chance to start over here."

"This woman is one of your office staffers?" Vanessa copied down the line entry in a notebook while Bliss pressed a button to print the whole file.

"She's been with me for six months," Bliss confirmed, typing in the user name to search the rest of the log for repeated visits. "A really bright girl with lots of potential, but she fell on hard times last year and got involved in an escort service to pay the bills."

Vanessa tapped the end of her pen on her notebook spiral. "Can you find out how many men she's been in contact with? We have reason to suspect her in a murder committed the Saturday before this past weekend."

Tempest hated the sick feeling in her belly that told her they were finally on the right track.

"It's difficult to trace this since clients can use their private e-mail accounts in addition to the temporary boxes set up through Blind Date." Bliss scanned her screen, shoulders slumping with the defeated look of someone who realizes how severely her trust had been misplaced. "But it looks like she's been in touch with at least three men."

Premonition turned to full-fledged icy dread.

"Is one of them KingKong?" Her voice caught on a hoarse note as she thought about Wes alone with a woman gone off the deep end.

Vanessa looked at her curiously but said nothing while Bliss squinted at the screen.

Tempest knew the answer when the woman paled.

"Yes. Do you think that's the screen name of the murder victim?"

Not yet.

Tempest ignored the fearful part of her that said they might already be too late to help Wes tonight. If ever there'd been a compelling reason to shove aside her fears and scrounge together all her courage, this was it. They had to reach Wes before Marianne Oakes struck again.

Perhaps reading her thoughts, Vanessa pulled Tempest to her feet and warned Bliss that she would be needed for questioning later that evening or the next day. Tempest barely heard the rest of their exchange as she remembered how Wes had been by her side when this person had crossed her path earlier in the week. She vowed this time, she would repay the favor and be there for Wes before anything happened to him.

"KingKong is the ID Wes is using?" Vanessa confirmed the fact with her before pulling out her cell phone as they left the penthouse suite and took the elevator down to street level.

"Yes." She was grateful Vanessa would know how to get in touch with Wes before they drove down to Mick's. The sooner they warned him, the better.

Distracted with worry, Tempest stumbled slightly to keep pace with Wes's supremely athletic partner as they hurried up the street. Squinting through the darkness in a canopied tunnel erected over a construction zone, Tempest listened for Vanessa's call to go through but lost sight of the other woman in the crush of people getting out of work for the day.

By the time she blinked her way back into the overcast haze of daylight along with the rest of the five o'clock pedestrian traffic, Tempest realized Vanessa was nowhere in sight.

Panic skittered over her. Hundreds of people shoved by her in their daily rush from work to home, yet Tempest couldn't remember ever feeling so utterly alone. Peering back into the construction tunnel, she saw no sign of Vanessa. She had vanished completely off a busy sidewalk.

Had something happened to her? Or had she simply jumped in the nearest cab, forgetting all about Wes's girlfriend of the month?

As much as she wanted to figure it out, Tempest was no detective. The person who would know how to help Vanessa was Wes, and right now she needed to reach him before Marianne Oakes got to him first.

Knowing she didn't stand a chance of hailing a cab at rush hour, Tempest stepped onto the first bus she saw, a 7th Avenue local that dropped her on 18th Street, only a few blocks from Mick's. She didn't think anyone had purposely followed her onto the bus, but public transportation overflowed with commuters at this time of day and there had been a crowd at the bus stop.

To be safe, she picked up speed as she walked through the lower West side, pedestrian traffic thinning out the farther west she went. After she passed 8th Avenue, the evening had turned completely dark with less street light to brighten the gloom. Just past 9th Avenue, the skies opened in a downpour that sent what few people had been on the streets back indoors.

Leaving Tempest running headlong through the cold, wet night alone.

Finally spying the awning for Mick's Grill, one of the few businesses with a storefront in a predominantly warehouse district, she peered over her shoulder into the dark, relieved to find the street empty for nearly half a block. Her heart had been racing for nothing.

Now she only needed to make sure Wes got the message about Marianne Oakes, and leave it up to him to decide what happened to Vanessa.

She'd wrestled with a guilty conscience ever since she hightailed it out of midtown where Wes's partner had disappeared, but Wes would know what to do. Hurrying past a row of windows outside of Mick's, she had almost reached the shelter of the awning when an iron hand clamped over her mouth.

14

WES TRIED TO BE SUBTLE as he checked his watch for the third time at a booth just inside the front door of Mick's Grill. His sixth date seemed like a nervous, self-conscious woman and he didn't want to give her any more reason to feel ill at ease, but the longer Vanessa went without answering her phone, the more he worried.

He'd tried Tempest's apartment three times and Vanessa's cell phone twice. No answer on either one.

Why did they have to leave Tempest's apartment in the first place? He told himself Vanessa could handle any trouble if they went to the market or ran a couple of errands, but they should have been back by now.

Unease crept down his spine along with restless tension. He peered out the window onto the street, his gaze chasing shadows while darkness cloaked the city. Reminding himself to pay attention to his date so he could finish up their meeting and call it a day, he decided to cancel his last two appointments so he could check on Tempest.

But as he wrenched his attention from the narrow

windows, he realized the woman across from him was staring outside with even more apprehension scrawled across her features than churned inside him.

"Everything okay?" The cop in him went on alert. The woman—Mary? Mary Anne?—hadn't said much since she sat down beyond a few cursory replies to questions he'd asked her. He hadn't given her any reason to be so nervous that the trembling of her hands caused the wine in her glass to vibrate with the force of it. "Did you want me to walk you to your car?"

"No!" The very idea seemed to startle her, propelling her out of her seat. She gathered her purse, a well-worn brown leather bag with a frayed handle. "I mean— Sorry we didn't hit it off right away, Wesley. Maybe we shouldn't take this any further."

She extended her hand, catching him off guard by leaving so suddenly. Was it him who made her nervous? Or did she have another reason for an obvious case of jitters?

He held up his hand in the classic surrender pose, hoping to put her at ease long enough to ask her a few more questions. His intuition started buzzing overtime. What if she knew something about his case? She *was* a blonde. Of course, half of his appointments today had been fair-haired as well.

Still, he couldn't afford to check on Vanessa and Tempest now if this was the woman he'd been searching for.

"I understand if you'd like to get going, but do you mind if I ask what's the rush?" He stared meaningfully at the distance between them across the table. "I'm not crowding you, right? And I swear I won't walk you to your car if you don't want me to. But I don't have anywhere else to go if our date doesn't work out tonight, so whether or not we hit if off, I've got nothing but time to talk."

With one more glance over her shoulder she sat back down, perching on the edge of her seat as if ready to take off at a moment's notice. "Maybe for another minute or two."

"Are you meeting someone else?" He couldn't imagine why else she'd need to check the front door so often. Leaning back into his seat, he kept his body posture unnaturally relaxed in an effort to gain her confidence.

As job duties went, Wes would rather take punches from a high-flying druggie right now than force himself to stay so still when tension tightened inside him.

But when she pulled a small inhaler free from her purse and took a long breath of some sort of medicine, he could tell he'd done the right thing in sticking around. He watched some of the tension slide out of her shoulders before she shook her head, her blond dye job shaking loose of the two chopsticks she'd used to hold it in place.

"No. I'm not meeting anyone. But I've got a psycho ex-boyfriend who likes to check up on me, and I really have no business drawing nice guys like you into my life until I figure out how to deal with him." She cast him an apologetic smile, her fingers trembling on the inhaler until she dropped it back into her purse.

A psycho boyfriend?

And with blinding clarity, Wes knew where to look for his murder suspect. He just didn't know how it tied into MatingGame or Tempest.

Lightning flashed outside the bar, the jagged bolt of brightness illuminating the window beside their table for an instant.

"Should I be worried?" He said it with a smile, but deep inside, he was already damn scared. Not for himself, because he could handle whatever came his way.

But, oh God, was he ever scared for Tempest.

"Not for yourself." Her expression changed, her eyes clouding faster than the stormy sky over Manhattan. "But he gets pretty pissed with me whenever I venture out without him. He's a mechanic with a lot of macho bullshit pride. Some guys just don't get the message, you know?"

He was about to ask her more about her ex-boyfriend—a mechanic might very well possess lockpicking skills—when something snagged his peripheral vision. A woman passed by the windowpane beside their table, a brief reflection of a familiar figure outside in the rain.

Tempest?

She was there one minute and then she was gone.

Shooting to his feet, he stepped back from the booth he'd shared with his latest blind date.

"Will you wait up just one minute, Mary?" He wanted to question the woman further, to find out what made her so edgy tonight, but if Tempest was here instead of her apartment, something must be very wrong.

He'd learned a long time ago not to question his instincts, and they were kicking into overdrive tonight. The cop buzz rattled his ears so loudly he felt as though he had a whole hive humming in his head. He didn't know what Mary's crazy ex-boyfriend could want with Tempest, but his gut told him that he'd been looking for a killer in all the wrong places for the last few days.

The murderer wasn't a woman who'd used MatingGame. It was a furious man who couldn't stand the idea of his girlfriend going out with anyone else. A man who killed anyone who got near his woman.

Darting through the happy-hour crowd that was even thicker tonight than the evening before, Wes wound his way to the exit and wrenched open the door. Rain poured down on the street outside, reflecting the bar lights and streetlights across the slick, shiny surfaces of cement sidewalk, blacktop road and brick buildings.

She was nowhere.

"Tempest." He shouted her name, startling two women sharing a cigarette under Mick's awning.

No reply. No sign of her or Vanessa. No sound but the sheeting rain that drowned out all other noises. He reached automatically for his cell phone and hit redial, hoping like hell he'd been wrong about seeing Tempest. Maybe she'd pick up her phone and he could just write off the vision of her in the bar's window as wishful thinking.

Instead, the phone rang and rang.

Something had gone wrong tonight. Massively,

horribly wrong. The realization body-slammed him like one of Vanessa's kung fu moves, scrambling his brain for one valuable instant and forcing him to acknowledge he would be devastated if anything happened to Tempest. He'd been wracked with guilt when Steve went missing, but this... It would level him completely.

Feet already in motion, he sprinted down the sidewalk in the direction he swore he'd seen her. He skidded to a halt in the alleyway where she'd flashed him just last night—her beautiful body full of life and so damn vulnerable.

Cold rain fell harder, pounding him with its wet weight in relentless sheets. Seeing nothing in the alley, he turned on his heel, ready to search the whole damn West side.

His foot crunched something on the pavement.

Bending, he picked up the object. A compact mirror.

Tossing the broken glass in a trash can, he continued back out into the street, slowing his pace enough to do a visual sweep of the sidewalk as he jogged.

And prayed.

She had to be safe, damn it. He wouldn't accept anything less. Couldn't conceive where he would be without her.

And as the rain pelted his brain, it seemed to drive home the message he'd been afraid to face.

He loved Tempest.

The simple truth blared out of him even as he faced a fear unlike anything he'd ever known. He'd been too much of a chickenshit to admit he'd felt something deep and real with her when she'd asked him. And now that he was faced with the prospect of never getting to tell her, the fact that he loved her seemed elementary. Fundamental to who he was and what he wanted in life.

Didn't matter that he'd known her for a handful of days. He'd fallen in love carefully—thoughtfully—in his past and made piss-poor decisions. Maybe it made a weird sort of sense that now—when he'd operated on blind instincts with someone he'd known for less than a week—he was positive he had it right.

But he'd never have the chance to tell her as much unless he found her. Fast.

He called for backup from his precinct, needing all the help he could scavenge when his whole world came down to the safety of one woman.

IT WOULDN'T BE a good night to die.

Tempest couldn't help but think all evidence of her murder would be wiped away in the downpour showering over her nightmare as she struggled against her captor dragging her past 11th Avenue toward the Hudson River. With one clammy palm clamped over her mouth, the man sealed her nose flat to her face, making breathing all but impossible. Screaming was out of the question.

The man who held her was so strong, his grip on her so ironclad, she imagined they looked like a couple running to get out of the rain with half his coat draped over her head. In reality, he had her stuffed inside his jacket to bind her even more tightly to his side, his knife jabbed convincingly against her right hip ever since he'd taken her. Had it been five minutes? Ten? It couldn't be much longer than that since they'd only walked a long block.

A monster of a human being—at least six foot five—her tormentor had grabbed her outside of Mick's Grill, moments before she would have reached Wes. Safety.

But she refused to think about that now when she needed to figure out how to get away. Back to Wes. He didn't deserve to have another woman forsake him, and she wouldn't let the psycho bastard who held her rob Wes of the chance to know how much she wanted him. How much she already regretted her decision to put off her happiness for the sake of independence.

She'd been doling out a few items from her purse to leave Wes clues à la Hansel and Gretel, but she needed to do more than that if she didn't want to end up as fish food for whatever creatures populated the Hudson River these days.

Scary, scary thought.

Right up there with never again seeing the lines around Wes's eyes crinkle up when he smiled.

She'd wanted her independence, right? What better time to prove to herself that she could be self-reliant? If she could break free of monster man, she would consider herself as kick-ass ready for life as any woman ever had been. And then, by God, if she survived this ordeal, she would embrace Wes Shaw with both hands and allow herself to be happy. Never again would she feel inferior to her poised and gorgeous mother or the dozens of people employed by Boucher Enterprises who seemed smarter and more efficient than her. She was Tempest Boucher, connoisseur of all things romantic, and that would damn well have to be enough.

Remembering a few self-defense moves from her kickboxing class, she dropped to her knees suddenly, going completely weightless in her captor's grip. He lost his hold on her, his big, meaty paw catching her hair awkwardly as she dashed away.

For about two seconds.

He caught up to her before she could fling herself in the headlight beam of an oncoming car, her desperate attempt to free herself foiled in no time.

"What the hell are you doing?" The man roared at her. It was the only way she could hear him over the unyielding din of the rain. "No one runs away from Luther."

Perhaps he wasn't worried any longer about someone seeing them in this warehouse district of the city because he brandished the knife in front of her as a warning. This part of the West side was deserted, with only a few abandoned buildings and burnt-out shops between them and the river.

She went still against him, frustrated that a total stranger could harbor so much fury toward her. Who was this man and how did he fit with Marianne Oakes? The lunatic's grip tightened around her rain-soaked clothing. Wes's trench coat around her shoulders provided her with little barrier between her and her captor, but it managed to comfort her on a mental level somehow, giving her a little extra strength.

"Why are you doing this?" Tempest shouted back at him without considering the wisdom of engaging in conversation with a crazy man. But maybe he'd get distracted if he started talking. She'd been so close to escape a minute ago. All she needed was a little more of a head start.

"I can't let my Marianne go back to spreading her legs for any guy with a few bucks to spare." He spoke close to her ear, his words angry and cold as he yanked her toward an abandoned gas station. "And I sure as hell can't allow the owner of her whorehouse to go unpunished. I tried to get you today in midtown, but I nailed the wrong damn woman."

Nailed? Dread pooled in her belly as she thought about Vanessa disappearing this afternoon. Had he shot her?

Fear froze Tempest from the inside out as she realized Marianne Oakes wasn't responsible for anyone's murder. It was this man who'd done the killing. A jealous boyfriend who'd come unhinged.

But no matter that she'd finally figured out the mystery, she'd never be able to share it with Wes at this rate. Luther's knife glinted dangerously close to her face again, a tangible reminder that her time was almost up unless she thought of something. Fast.

Too bad the only thing that came to mind was how much she loved Wes Shaw.

With that realization making her more determined than ever to get away, she reached into her purse with her free hand and flicked out the last remaining object. The newspaper photo of her with Wes.

She watched the clipping float down to the pavement for an instant before it succumbed to the deluge, a wet piece of paper plastered to the concrete, no doubt smudged beyond recognition.

WES DIDN'T HAVE a clue where he was going.

He raced through the darkness after disconnecting his distress call to the police dispatcher. They'd send somebody as soon they could.

Probably not soon enough.

Cursing the city's permanently overtaxed department, Wes knew his own efforts would have to be enough this time. He just needed his instincts to kick in. Anytime now, damn it.

Slipping on a piece of paper, he paused long enough to make out the slick magazine-style cover of *Soap Opera Digest,* a trio of glitzy daytime TV stars grinning up at him to mock his total lack of understanding when it came to Tempest.

Or to give him a new direction?

Soap Opera Digest couldn't have been lying in the street for too long since the inside pages weren't soaked yet. Instinct—or the hopeful imaginings of a man in need of a second chance—told him Tempest had dropped it there to give him a lead.

Scanning the street, he searched the rain-slicked darkness for more hints that she'd been here. The deluge hit the pavement so hard it drowned out the rumble of traffic two blocks away, filling his ears with blaring white noise that stifled all other sounds.

Would it drown her out if she cried out? Fear pummeled him at the thought of Tempest alone and vulnerable. Where the hell was Vanessa tonight?

Trying not to assume the worst, he told himself she had to have been nearby. No way would a second partner let him down.

He drew his gun—a Smith & Wesson 9 mm he'd be all too glad to fire tonight—and hastened his step. Even in the darkness, his searching gaze picked out a comb, a gum wrapper that may or may not have been hers and a sopping newspaper clipping of him and Tempest when they'd been photographed together outside her offices.

She'd saved it.

Love for her funneled through him, fueling his steps even when the bread crumb trail of her belongings disappeared outside a deserted gas station near the Hudson. The perfect isolated place to commit a crime.

Jamming the wet assortment of Tempest's belongings in his pants pocket, he raised his gun higher and swallowed back the mixture of fear and fury tangling inside him. Ran like hell for the old Shell station. If the rain impaired his hearing, it would keep Tempest's captor at a disadvantage, too.

Finding the front door locked, he eased around the back to look for a window.

And discovered two figures struggling on the pavement behind the building. A man bent over a woman's prone body.

Tempest's body.

Horror washed through him—a cold, endless

wave that sucked out his backbone and left him weak in the knees. But he refused to acknowledge the possibility that anything had happened to her for more than a split second. With a roar of fury, Wes charged the guy as he saw the flash of a blade at Tempest's throat.

Her attacker never saw him coming—he was preoccupied with threatening a woman who rescued stray dogs from trash cans when she wasn't romanticizing the world with her sculptures.

Son of a—

Wes hit him like a freight train, directing all his fury toward her assailant. The guy's head met the blacktop beneath Wes's chest as Wes rolled over him with continued momentum. The knife dropped to the ground, the discordant clank of metal sounding through the downpour.

He forced himself to limit his gun use to a crack across her attacker's temple, coldcocking the bastard into last year. But if he found out the guy had hurt her...

"Wes?" Tempest shouted behind him, her voice soothing a raw wound inside him.

Whipping around, he saw her slowly coming to her knees, her clothes covered in dirt and mud.

"You're okay." He told her instead of asking her, willing it to be so. "Are you okay?"

He couldn't go to her until he'd cuffed the guy who could only be the jealous boyfriend of the woman he'd been sitting with at Mick's. Still, Wes dragged him to a rusted sign pole and secured his wrists on either side so that he could help Tempest.

Pocketing the keys, he finally heard the squeal of police sirens in the distance, the rain slowing enough so that he could hear more than his own heart beating.

"Vanessa disappeared in midtown." Tempest swiped a blotch of mud from her cheek and straightened the skirt she wore beneath Wes's trench coat, which he only just realized he must have left at her place for the second time.

He helped her up off the ground, so damn grateful to have reached her in time. Smoothing his hands over her face, her neck, her shoulders, he reassured himself she wasn't hurt.

And then her words began to sink in.

"What do you mean *disappeared?*" He'd trusted Vanessa to watch over Tempest. She wouldn't neglect her job unless... "Something must have happened to her."

Nodding, she pursed her lips and winced as a result of the cut on her mouth. He hadn't seen it before with a swath of dirt across her chin, but now that the slowing rain washed it away he could see her lower lip was split, the swollen flesh dripping a narrow track of blood.

Regret stung him that she had to be dragged into this at all. Vanessa should have protected her, damn it.

"*He* did something to her." She didn't need to point. She tracked an accusing gaze toward her attacker. "I don't know what, but while he was dragging me down the street he said something about following us after we left Bliss's—"

"Who's Bliss?" Where were those squad cars? He needed to get Tempest somewhere safe and find Vanessa before this case exploded any further in his face.

He told himself this wasn't a replay of two years ago when his first partner had gone missing. Vanessa was better than that. Stronger than that.

And damn it, he trusted her. Whatever had happened today must have been pretty bad to wipe out his ninja backup who'd never let him down.

Before Tempest could answer, he put in another call to dispatch to provide their exact location, since they'd come a long way from Mick's Grill. Although he had every intention of finding Vanessa, his first priority was getting Tempest—the woman he loved—to safety.

Once he hung up the phone, she related the events that had taken place earlier in the day when she and Vanessa unearthed the source of the call girl rumors. He couldn't help but admire Tempest's determination to wrest answers from the MatingGame operations manager, but his main concern now was finding his partner.

"So Vanessa vanished after you left this woman's house?" Wes waved over the police car that finally found them in the rain outside the forsaken Shell station.

"We went into one of those wooden tunnels they put up around construction sites and—"

"Shaw." A uniformed officer burst from the arriving police car before it came to a stop. "Detective Torres just checked in. She got rolled in midtown and the guy took her phone."

Relief swept through him, making him feel stronger. Taller. And more certain of his judgment than ever. Vanessa hadn't betrayed him.

"She's okay?" He slid an arm around Tempest's waist, surprised how much the feel of her could bolster him. More than anything, he wanted to get her alone. To explore every inch of her firsthand to make sure she hadn't been hurt.

The officer nodded while his partner frisked Luther. "Torres is pissed about letting someone get the drop on her, but other than that she sounded okay." He jerked a thumb toward Tempest's attacker. "Was this the guy who did it?"

Another squad car pulled up and two more officers stepped out. The back door of the car opened more slowly, revealing...

"Vanessa." Wes's grip tightened on Tempest, but he didn't move to help his partner, not even when she wove a bit drunkenly on her feet through the last of the slowing raindrops.

He knew his ninja colleague well enough to know she'd probably drop-kick him if he offered her a hand.

Vanessa held a blood-spattered handkerchief to her temple, her color pale, but her eyes seemed focused and alert.

"I screwed up, Wes." She moved closer slowly, her gaze scanning the gas station parking lot enveloped in thick mist as the rain slowed to a stop. She watched the officers bagging the assailant's knife and reading him his rights. "I let myself get too caught up in the investigation and I took my eyes off her to call you."

Relief poured over him. Sure he was frustrated Vanessa had taken Tempest out of the safety of her apartment, but she was entitled to make mistakes. She'd done her best, and he couldn't reasonably ask for anything more.

Especially since she looked like she'd be carrying around some serious guilt about the incident for a long time. Her normally proud shoulders slumped with the weight of the mistake.

"You did what you could." Wes watched the other officers haul the attacker to his feet. "And bottom line, we've got our killer in custody."

Tempest watched Wes try to cheer Vanessa and admired the way he tried to lessen the woman's sense of responsibility. Still, guilt nipped Tempest as she wondered if she should have done something differently after they'd left Bliss's apartment earlier that day. Should she have spent more time looking for Vanessa?

She moved out of Wes's arm to look at Vanessa's head.

"What happened to you anyhow? You were a few feet in front of me and then you disappeared in the rush hour crunch." She brushed aside the other woman's long dark hair to inspect the cut.

Her own muscles ached from being hauled through the lower West side by a madman. Her feet burned from a hundred little places where her skin had been rubbed raw against the pavement, but none of her injuries seemed significant next to the laceration on Vanessa's temple.

"I heard a noise in the construction tunnel."

Vanessa winced as Tempest picked a few strands from the drying blood caked around the wound. "The guy probably just whistled to get my attention. But as I turned into the outlet that connected the tunnel to the subway to wait for Tempest and check out the noise, I got nailed in the head with something."

Tempest watched the mixture of emotions cross Wes's face—anger, worry, the need for vengeance. She didn't know how she'd missed so many feelings within the man before—when he'd asked her to give them another chance—but she could see them now.

And knew she had a lot more to learn about Wesley Shaw.

One of the uniformed officers jogged over to them, carrying some kind of black handle with a leather strap attached to it. "Guy's name is Luther Murray and he just admitted to winging you with a slingshot." He brandished the weapon that looked like something a caveman would use, along with a Ziploc bag of small silver balls. "The ammo isn't high tech, but I bet it could do some serious damage."

"Great," Vanessa muttered. "Knocked unconscious by a kid's toy. Thanks, Collins."

"You'd better get this stitched up, Vanessa." Tempest told herself she would not be queasy from the sight of someone else's wound. Vanessa had taken the hit because she'd been protecting *her,* after all. The least she could do was offer a little support before she fainted from the sight of all that blood.

And the thought of how much worse the injury could have been.

Vanessa nodded, swiping away a trickle of blood sliding down her cheek. "Will do. But I had to see if Wes needed help first."

Tempest could see the wealth of anguish in the other woman's eyes and she would be willing to gamble it had little to do with the gaping gash just below her hairline. Vanessa simply hated letting Wes down.

"Thanks, Torres." Wes leaned in to clap her on the shoulder before he stepped back to sling an arm around Tempest again. "I found her, and that's all that matters. My last date at Mick's tipped me off when she mentioned a jealous boyfriend who didn't want her dating anyone else, but I couldn't figure out why this woman's ex would trash Tempest's place until she told me about MatingGame hiring former prostitutes."

Tempest watched a dazed Luther ride away in the back of one of the police cars, amazed to find herself still standing strong by Wes's side even after facing abduction. A knife. The threat of missing out on a second chance with Wes.

She didn't know which had scared her the most, but she did know she'd survived to embrace her future with both hands. The time she'd spent keeping herself alive with Luther Murray's knife pressed to her neck had assured her she had deeper reserves of strength than she would have ever guessed.

"Tempest helped me see the connection when she knew your screen name, KingKong." Vanessa gave Wes a soft slug in the arm while the two remaining police officers waited by their squad car, the lights silently flashing through the mist. "She'd make a hell of a partner for someone who deserved her."

Touched that Vanessa seemed to have forgiven her for taking off after she disappeared, Tempest smiled back. She also appreciated the good word of mouth with Wes since she wanted him to see her that way— as a genuine partner and not just a spoiled socialite in need of protection.

Winking with her good eye, Vanessa walked backward toward the squad car. "Besides, I've got an appointment with the E.R. to make sure I don't have a BB pellet lodged in my gray matter."

"That's right. The invincible ninja was taken down by stone age know-how." Wes flashed her a grin as she slid into the car. "You'd better rest up for all the grief you're going to get around the precinct for this one."

Rolling her eyes, Vanessa settled in the back of the police car while one of the officers in the front seat called over to them. "You need a ride, Shaw?"

"Hell, no. I'm taking my own sweet time to get back to the station because I damn well earned myself some slack today. I'll be there as soon as we can scrounge up some dry clothes."

The vehicle pulled away, leaving Tempest and Wes alone in the heavy white mist, which was turning gradually to big, fat snowflakes.

"Are you sure we didn't want that ride?" Tempest blew on her hands to thaw them, her outfit soaked and chilled despite Wes's trench coat around her shoulders.

Wes pulled her closer, tucking her hands inside his jacket. "I wanted you all to myself for five minutes before we head over to the station. You know you're going to have to come with me since I need to take your statement about what happened today?"

Warmth flowed through her at the tender concern in his eyes, the gentle way he touched her. By some miracle, she'd won her second chance with Wes and she didn't have any intention of blowing it.

"Fine by me since I have a lot of statements I want to make to you, Detective."

15

WES GOT HIS SECOND WIND at the precinct two hours later as he typed up his final report for the night.

He'd stuck around long enough to hear Marianne Oakes's tearful apology for using the MatingGame dating service, and the pieces to the puzzle had finally all fallen into place in his mind. Apparently Marianne was too scared of her ex-boyfriend to hit the bars around her home at night or to meet men in the New York dating scene, so she'd hoped Blind Date might help her meet people anonymously in remote locations Luther Murray wouldn't find.

Even Wes's chief of detectives, a hard-boiled cop who'd seen the worst the city had to offer, seemed to sympathize with the former hooker. Especially when her mother showed up at the station with Marianne's three-year-old daughter. Bliss Holloway might have opened a can of worms by hiring an ex-prostitute looking for a way out, but Wes could appreciate the woman's desire to give people a second chance.

Then again, maybe Wes had a particular soft place in his heart tonight for second chances, since his thoughts never strayed far from Tempest and all the ways he wanted to make things work between them. He'd given her the high-pressure pitch earlier that day, thinking he needed to sell her on a relationship before she booted him out of her life for good. But now that he realized he loved her and the feelings he had for her weren't ever going to go away, he didn't see the need to push her into something she wasn't ready for yet.

He'd still be crazy about her tomorrow and next week and next year. She'd get the idea sooner or later, and frankly, he had all the time in the world to wait.

For that matter, maybe he'd get another tattoo. Only this time, he wouldn't put it around his wrist like a ball and chain to keep him tied down. He'd scrawl her name right over his heart where she'd already made a permanent place for herself.

Closing his eyes while he saved his document in progress, he savored the thought of Tempest in his life. His imagination was so strong, so vivid, he swore he could smell her sweet almond fragrance.

"Can we blow this clambake, Detective?" Her voice cut through his thoughts as she leaned over his shoulder to peer at his computer. "I've already given my statement and MatingGame has been cleared of any wrongdoing."

"We?" Anticipation fired through him at the thought of them together for a little longer tonight. He clicked Send on the report before shutting down the computer for the night. "I hope that means you're going to let me drive you home."

Tempest let his words slide over her, grateful for

the sound of his voice and the warmth of his presence after those terrifying moments when she'd feared she'd never have another chance to be with him. She pulled his damp suit jacket off the back of his office chair and handed it to him. Although he'd asked their cabdriver to stop off at Tempest's apartment so she could get some dry clothes on the way to the precinct, he hadn't taken time to change.

Always putting her needs first.

"I've been waiting for a chance to talk to you alone." She stared up into his eyes, remembering that Friday night he'd calmly strolled into the mayhem of her life and helped her restore some order. Her priorities had crystallized since then, her focus narrowing to the things—and people—most important to her. "Besides, Vanessa left Kong at my place. She and Eloise have been alone there for half the day."

"Then I'm definitely driving you home." He shrugged his way into his jacket and retrieved his car keys from a desk drawer. "They've either destroyed your place or they're waking up the neighbors with howls for food. You know how much Kong eats in a day?"

Leaving the building, they found the city streets covered in snow. Tempest took pleasure in holding on to Wes's arm while they slipped and slid their way to his car, but as they drove the handful of blocks to her apartment, she was surprised how quiet he'd become.

For days, there'd been so much to say, so much ground to cover for his case. And now...there wasn't anything left to talk about except for what was happening between them.

Deciding she'd waited long enough to dive into those dark, emotional waters, Tempest was ready to take the plunge when Wes spoke up from the driver's seat.

"Is this Bliss woman going to be in trouble with the company after she went out on a limb to help Marianne?" He pulled into a parking space on the street in front of her building, carefully avoiding a few teenagers lobbing snowball bombs at each other from the safety of parked cars.

"We do need to standardize hiring practices at Boucher, but I like the idea of leveraging company profits to help people in the city who need it most." She'd been thinking a lot about what Bliss had tried to do since the woman's efforts really resonated with her. "Before I step down as CEO, I'd like to change our corporate mission to reflect some charitable efforts. Maybe then I can tell myself that these past few months of company reorganization will have lasting effects that won't fade away just because I'm not in the driver's seat anymore."

"I bet you could do a lot of good with the excess profits." Wes steadied her with his arm as they made their way to the door of her building. "Maybe Kelly Kline won't want to quit once she sees what a forward-thinking company she's working for."

Tempest brushed the snow from her shoulders as they stepped inside and called the elevator. "Something tells me her threat of resignation was just a stunt to make me recognize her value." She suppressed a little shiver of anticipation as Wes entered the elevator with her. The confined space made her all too aware of how much she wanted to resolve the problems between them—and take advantage of the heat that simmered close to the surface. "But she's very good at what she does, so if she doesn't mind supporting the new Boucher mission, I'm glad to have her stay on board."

"The more money she makes, the more money you can spend on worthy causes." Wes remained on his side of the elevator while she stayed on hers, a yawning ache of space between them.

She would fix that, just as soon as they reached the privacy of her apartment. "What better excuse for capitalism at its shameless best?"

"And no need to feel guilty about revenues you're only giving back to the community." Wes stood aside while she disarmed the lock and opened the door to her apartment. "I don't know what your mother will think of the plan, but I really admire you for making the effort."

"Thank you." Her heart warmed to his praise, and she couldn't remember the last time anyone had told her they were proud of anything she'd done. She'd taken pride in her sculptures. And she'd been glad that she held Boucher Enterprises together for eight months without incident, but no one else in her life had ever shared the sentiment.

Still, even though Wes's praise meant a lot to her, Tempest realized she didn't need it to feel strong and secure about herself. She'd waited a lifetime for her mother to dole out a few gentle words, and never again would she pin her self-worth on what anyone else thought about her. Tonight she'd proven to herself that she was made of sterner stuff than she'd ever imagined.

Soft, tired woofs greeted them as Kong and Eloise lifted their heads from the throw rug in the middle of the living room. There was no mess, no signs of massive destruction. Only a shared pillow on the floor where both dogs lowered their big, furry heads before falling back asleep.

"Somebody made herself at home today." Wes bent to give his dog a scratch on the head. "I don't know how I'm going to pry Kong out of here without a fight."

"Then maybe you should make yourself comfortable, too." Tempest figured she owed it to him to spell out what she wanted since she'd been the one with cold feet the last time they talked about any kind of future together.

He stared back at her in the dark apartment lit only by a night-light she liked to leave on for Eloise.

"I'm not sure that would be a good idea." Straightening, he ran his hand along the back of his neck. "I know myself well enough to be pretty certain I can't manage a sleepover without the intimacy. That kind of sensitivity just isn't in my genetic makeup. But that's not to say I couldn't handle it somewhere down the road."

She was still reeling from his polite refusal to spend the night when his last words penetrated her consciousness. "You would give me…more time?"

"Isn't that what you wanted? Some space to straighten out your own life before you think about getting wound up in mine?"

Her heart did a skip-hop in her chest, an off balance beat that reminded her how much she needed to share with him.

Drawing him deeper into the studio apartment, she held one of his hands in hers, thinking she wouldn't let him leave until she'd told him everything important. Everything that mattered.

"I *thought* I needed more time." She'd woken up this morning so scared of the future, so worried that she'd never be able to forge her own way in the world with a strong, take-charge man in her life. "But what I failed to realize is that my life will never be perfect. There will never be a supremely comfortable time to have a relationship because there will always be problems to overcome, a career to worry about or a character flaw to obsess over."

"So you're saying there will never be a good time for us?" His hand squeezed both of hers, smoky gray eyes searching hers in the dim night-light from the range hood a few feet away in her kitchen.

"No, I'm saying I need to stop romanticizing the way people fall in love and just remind myself I'm already there. Whether or not I've gotten my life squared away, the truth is I'm crazy about you *now*, Wesley Shaw. I love you and I don't want to wait for all our stars to be perfectly aligned before I get brave enough to take a chance with—"

She might have stumbled on with words for another half hour if Wes hadn't slanted his lips over hers and kissed her with all the warmth she felt in her heart.

He slid an arm around her waist, lifting her

against him as he pressed her back to the living room wall. He tasted her with a thoroughness that left her weak. Mindless. Hungry for more.

When he broke the kiss, it was only long enough to whisper in her ear.

"I'm in love with you, Tempest."

Ooh.

She wrapped her arms around his neck and held on for dear life as he kissed her again. Staggering with the pleasurable weight of that news, she felt overwhelmed this amazing man could love a neurotic artist trapped in the public eye wearing a business suit.

Easing back, she cupped his jaw with her palm. "Are you sure? Because if you fell in love with the corporate chick on the conference room desk, I have to tell you that wasn't the real me."

"No?" He didn't look terribly concerned. In fact, amusement danced in his eyes as he roamed his hands over her hips and around to her back.

"No. The real me is the soap-opera-watching junk-food junkie." She bit her lip for a moment, wondering how to define herself to this man who had only met her in crisis mode. "I like to ride my bike when I walk my dog and reporters with cameras scare me. I like to create naked sculptures of men and just as soon as I find the right person to head up Boucher Enterprises, I'm leaving behind the corporate world to work on my art full-time."

"Don't worry." He leaned in to nip her ear and soothe the bite with a lazy sweep of his tongue. "I love that woman, too. And maybe if you're a self-employed artist, you won't mind the crazy hours of a cop."

"I promise I can handle the police work. Even if it involves an occasional prostitution bust." A new sense of peace flowed over her, a dose of confidence she hadn't expected from being in love. "Although I may ask you to do some overtime nude modeling for me during your off hours so I can reassure myself how much you want me."

She allowed her hands to roam over his crotch, already feeling very reassured.

"I think I can handle the extra work." He pulled away from her, holding her at arm's length to study her. "But wait a minute. Do you think this new artistic woman wears blindfolds like the corporate chick used to?"

"Oh, I think she can be convinced." She ran her hands over his chest, soaking up the solid strength of him. "I have the feeling she likes playing all sorts of games."

"Sounds like my kind of woman." Wes toyed with the buttons of her blouse, taking his time undoing each one and igniting a wealth of heat deep inside her. "I wonder how she feels about visits to the tattoo parlor."

She arched her back to melt deeper into his touch. "After tonight, I'm guessing she's had enough brushes with sharp objects to last her a lifetime, but maybe if you held her hand…"

"No, she only needs to hold *my* hand since I'm the one going under another needle." He guided her hand to his chest, cradling her fingers against his shirt pocket until she felt the beat of his pulse. "Tempest the romantic deserves a big, red heart. Right here."

Touched more than she could say, Tempest led him toward the bed she wanted to share with him tonight and many more nights to come. Tugging him down to the pullout sofa, she could already see the years of walking their dogs and playing blindfold games rolling out in front of them.

"I think she's going to be very happy right there." She brushed a kiss over his heart, imagining his new tattoo. "Forever."

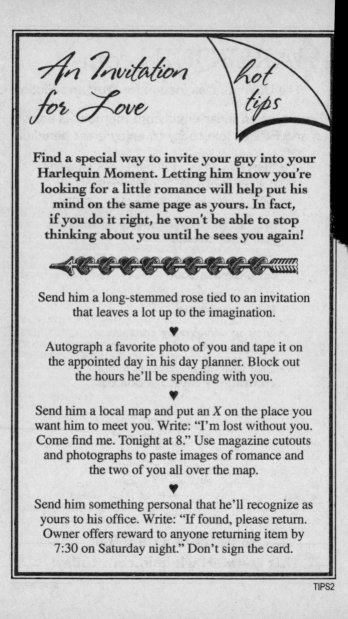

An Invitation for Love

hot tips

Find a special way to invite your guy into your Harlequin Moment. Letting him know you're looking for a little romance will help put his mind on the same page as yours. In fact, if you do it right, he won't be able to stop thinking about you until he sees you again!

Send him a long-stemmed rose tied to an invitation that leaves a lot up to the imagination.

♥

Autograph a favorite photo of you and tape it on the appointed day in his day planner. Block out the hours he'll be spending with you.

♥

Send him a local map and put an *X* on the place you want him to meet you. Write: "I'm lost without you. Come find me. Tonight at 8." Use magazine cutouts and photographs to paste images of romance and the two of you all over the map.

♥

Send him something personal that he'll recognize as yours to his office. Write: "If found, please return. Owner offers reward to anyone returning item by 7:30 on Saturday night." Don't sign the card.

Harlequin on Location

hot tips

Wherever your dream date location, pick a setting and a time that won't be interrupted by your daily responsibilities. This is a special time together. Here are a few hopelessly romantic settings to inspire you—they might as well be ripped right out of a Harlequin romance novel!

Bad weather can be so good.

Take a walk together after a fresh snowfall or when it's just stopped raining. Pick a snowball (or a puddle) fight, and see how long it takes to get each other soaked to the bone. Then enjoy drying off in front of a fire, or perhaps surrounded by lots and lots of candles with yummy hot chocolate to warm things up.

Candlelight dinner for two...in the bedroom.

Romantic music and candles will instantly transform the place you sleep into a cozy little love nest, perfect for nibbling. Why not lay down a blanket and open a picnic basket at the foot of your bed? Or set a beautiful table with your finest dishes and glowing candles to set the mood. Either way, a little bubbly and lots of light finger foods will make this a meal to remember.

A Wild and Crazy Weeknight.

Do something unpredictable...on a weeknight straight from work. Go to an art opening, a farm-team baseball game, the local playhouse, a book signing by an author or a jazz club—anything but the humdrum blockbuster movie. There's something very romantic about being a little wild and crazy—or at least out of the ordinary—that will bring out the flirt in both of you. And you won't be able to resist thinking about each other in anticipation of your hot date...or telling everyone the day after.

Looking for a seductive cocktail?

hot tips

Try *Ero-Desiac*—
a dazzling martini

With its warm apricot walls yet cool atmosphere, Verlaine is quickly becoming one of New York's hottest nightspots. Verlaine created a light, subtle yet seductive martini for Harlequin: the Ero-Desiac. Sake warms the heart and soul, while jasmine and passion fruit ignite the senses....

The Ero-Desiac

Combine vodka, sake, passion fruit puree and jasmine tea. Mix and shake. Strain into a martini glass, then rest pomegranate syrup on the edge of the martini glass and drizzle the syrup down the inside of the glass.